Ben Jonson's The Magnetic Lady, or Humors Reconciled (1632): A Retelling

David Bruce

Published by David Bruce, 2022.

BEN JONSON'S THE MAGNETIC LADY, OR HUMORS RECONCILED (1632): A RETELLING

First edition. July 14, 2022.

Copyright © 2022 David Bruce.

ISBN: 979-8201426200

Written by David Bruce.

Table of Contents

CAST OF CHARACTERS...1
THE INDUCTION, OR CHORUS...3
CHAPTER 1 | — 1.1 —..12
— 1.2 —...17
— 1.3 —...21
— 1.4 —...24
— 1.5 —...28
— 1.6 —...34
— 1.7 —...37
— CHORUS 1 —..42
CHAPTER 2 | — 2.1 —..46
— 2.2 —...48
— 2.3 —...52
— 2.4 —...57
— 2.5 —...60
— 2.6 —...65
— 2.7 —...75
— CHORUS 2 —..77
CHAPTER 3 | — 3.1 —..81
— 3.2 —...85
— 3.3 —...89
— 3.4 —...97
— 3.5 —...103
— 3.6 —...114
— CHORUS 3 —..117
CHAPTER 4 | — 4.1 —..119
— 4.2 —...120
— 4.3 —...124
— 4.4 —...128
— 4.5 —...132
— 4.6 —...134
— 4.7 —...138
— 4.8 —...142

— CHORUS 4 — 147

CHAPTER 5 | — 5.1 — 149

— 5.2 — 151

— 5.3 — 154

— 5.4 — 157

— 5.5 — 159

— 5.6 — 162

— 5.7 — 164

— 5.8 — 169

— 5.9 — 172

— 5.10 — 174

— CHORUS 5, AND EPILOGUE — | CHORUS 5, changed into an epilogue to the King 183

— NOTES — 184

— 1.4 — 186

— 2.3 — 189

— 2.6 — 190

— Chorus 2 — 192

— 3.1 — 196

— 3.1 — 198

— 3.5 — 200

— 3.5 — 201

— 3.5 — 202

— 4.7 — 203

— 4.8 — 204

— 5.7 — 205

— 5.7 — 206

APPENDIX A: FAIR USE 209

APPENDIX B: ABOUT THE AUTHOR 210

APPENDIX C: SOME BOOKS BY DAVID BRUCE.....................211

Dedicated to Carl Eugene Bruce and Josephine Saturday Bruce

***

Educate Yourself

Read Like A Wolf Eats

Be Excellent to Each Other

Books Then, Books Now, Books Forever

***

In this retelling, as in all my retellings, I have tried to make the work of literature accessible to modern readers who may lack some of the knowledge about mythology, religion, and history that the literary work's contemporary audience had.

Do you know a language other than English? If you do, I give you permission to translate this book, copyright your translation, publish or self-publish it, and keep all the royalties for yourself. (Do give me credit, of course, for the original retelling.)

I would like to see my retellings of classic literature used in schools, so I give permission to the country of Finland (and all other countries) to buy one copy of this eBook and give copies to all students forever. I also give permission to the state of Texas (and all other states) to buy one copy of this eBook and give copies to all students forever. I also give permission to all teachers to buy one copy of this eBook and give copies to all students forever.

Teachers need not actually teach my retellings. Teachers are welcome to give students copies of my eBooks as background material. For example, if they are teaching Homer's *Iliad* and *Odyssey*, teachers are welcome to give students copies of my *Virgil's* Aeneid: *A Retelling in Prose* and tell students, "Here's another ancient epic you may want to read in your spare time."

CAST OF CHARACTERS

LADY LOADSTONE *the magnetic lady; a loadstone is a magnet (something that attracts)*

MISTRESS POLISH *her gossip (friend and companion) and she-parasite*

PLACENTIA STEEL *her niece; the Latin word* placere *means "to give pleasure"*

PLEASANCE *her waiting-woman and daughter of Polish*

MISTRESS KEEP *the niece's nurse. She is an old woman.*

MOTHER CHAIR *the midwife. She is an old woman.*

MASTER COMPASS *a scholar mathematic*

CAPTAIN IRONSIDE *a soldier*

PARSON PALATE *prelate of the parish*

DOCTOR RUT *physician to the house*

TIM ITEM *his apothecary*

SIR DIAPHANOUS SILKWORM *a courtier, a viscount*

MASTER PRACTICE *a lawyer. "Practice" can mean a trick or scheme.*

SIR MOTH INTEREST *a usurer, aka money-bawd, and brother to Lady Loadstone*

MASTER BIAS *a vi-politic [vice-politician, aka assistant to an official], or sub-secretary. He engages in political manipulation on behalf of another person. He is an assistant to a politician. According to the* Oxford English Dictionary, *one meaning of politician is "A schemer or plotter; a shrewd, sagacious, or crafty person."*

MASTER NEEDLE *the lady's steward and tailor*

A FOOTBOY *a boy-servant*

A VARLET *an official with the power to make arrests*

CHORUS *by way of Induction*

MASTER PROBEE *the Latin word* probare *means "to approve"; the name suggests "probity" (honesty and decentness)*

MASTER DAMPLAY *an audience member who can damn a play without having understood it*

Note: Master Probee is an example of a member of the intelligent audience whom Ben Jonson hopes will see and enjoy his play. Master Damplay is an example of a member of the unintelligent audience whom Ben Jonson dislikes.

JOHN TRYGUST *boy of the house; he is a book-holder or prompter who helps actors when they forget their lines. "Trygust" means "Test Taste." Plays tend to test the taste of audience members. Will they recognize a good play when they see it?*

THE SCENE: LONDON
NOTES:
A compass is a device that uses magnetism to find the direction north.

A compass is also a device used to draw circles.

This society believed that the mixture of four humors in the body determined one's temperament. One humor could be predominant. The four humors are blood, yellow bile, black bile, and phlegm. If blood is predominant, then the person is sanguine (active, optimistic). If yellow bile is predominant, then the person is choleric (angry, bad-tempered). If black bile is predominant, then the person is melancholic (sad). If phlegm is predominant, then the person is phlegmatic (calm, apathetic, indolent).

Humors are dominant personality characteristics. For example, a person could be optimistic, or angry, or melancholic, or calm, or something else.

A humor can also be a fancy or a whim.

The word "humor" was an in-vogue word in Ben Jonson's day.

In Ben Jonson's society, a person of higher rank would use "thou," "thee," "thine," and "thy" when referring to a person of lower rank. (These terms were also used affectionately and between equals.) A person of lower rank would use "you" and "your" when referring to a person of higher rank.

"Sirrah" was a title used to address someone of a social rank inferior to the speaker. Friends, however, could use it to refer to each other.

The word "wench" in Ben Jonson's time was not necessarily negative. It was often used affectionately.

A "gossip" is a friend or companion or neighbor.

THE INDUCTION, OR CHORUS

Two gentlemen, Master Probee and Master Damplay, walked onto the stage.

A boy named John Trygust, who worked at the theater, met them.

"What do you lack, gentlemen?" he asked them. "What is it you need?"

This was the cry of shopkeepers as they tried to sell things to passersby.

John Trygust continued, "Any fine fancies, figures of speech, humors, characters, ideas, descriptions of lords and ladies?"

Humors are dominant personality characteristics. For example, a person could be optimistic, or angry, or melancholic, or calm, or something else.

John Trygust continued, "Waiting-women, parasites, knights, captains, courtiers, lawyers? What do you lack?"

Parasites are people who live on the wealth of other people.

Plays can supply all of the characters whom John Trygust was offering to the two gentlemen.

"He is a pretty prompt boy for the poetic shop," Probee said about the boy.

The boy was the prompter for actors who forgot their lines, and he was a prompter trying to get more audience members to see the play.

Damplay said, "And he is a bold boy!"

He then asked, "Where's one of your masters, sirrah? Where is the poet?"

Ben Jonson regarded playwrights as poets. In Elizabethan and Jacobean and Carolinian England, many plays included much poetry in the dialogue.

"Which of them?" John Trygust asked. "Sir, we have several poets who drive that trade now: poets, poetaccios, poetasters, poetitos —"

"Poetaccios, poetasters, poetitos" all are words used for poor, paltry poets.

"And all haberdashers of small wit, I presume," Damplay said.

Haberdashers dealt with small items that were used in sewing.

Damplay was critical of poets and of plays.

He then said, "We would speak with the poet of the day, boy."

The poet of the day was the playwright whose play would be performed that day. That playwright was Ben Jonson, author of *The Magnetic Lady*.

"Sir, he is not here," John Trygust said. "But I have the dominion and management of the shop for this time under him, and I can show you all the variety the stage will afford for the present.

"Therein you will express your own good qualities, boy," Probee said.

"And tie us two and make us indebted to you for the gentle office," Damplay said.

"We are a pair of public persons, this gentleman and myself, who are sent thus coupled to you upon state business," Probee said.

"Public persons" concern themselves with promoting the well-being of the public. The public is better off if good plays rather than bad plays are performed.

"It concerns only the state of the stage, I hope!" John Trygust said.

In this society, some playwrights were accused of putting political sedition in their plays. If found guilty, such playwrights could be severely punished.

"Oh, you shall know that by degrees, boy," Damplay said.

"No man leaps into a business of state without fording — crossing over — first the state of the business."

"Business" can mean 1) commerce, and 2) political affairs.

In other words: No man leaps into a commerce of state without fording — crossing over — first the state of the political affairs.

Also in other words: Playwrights need to be concerned about making a profit. To do that, they need to avoid having their play suppressed because of suspected seditious political content.

"We are sent to you, indeed, from the people," Probee said.

"The people!" John Trygust said. "Which side of the people?"

Liberals or conservatives? House of Peers or House of Commons? Government or the Loyal Opposition? Wealthy or impoverished?

When it comes to politics, much is uncertain, and a playwright may err and be accused of sedition.

"The venison side, if you know it, boy," Damplay said.

Venison comes from a deer, aka hart. The heart beats more strongly on the left side of the body.

"That's the left side," John Trygust said. "I had rather they had been the right."

The left side is the sinister side. *Sinister* is Latin for "left."

"So they are," Probee said. "Not the faeces [sediment] or grounds of your people, who sit in the oblique caves and wedges of your house, your sinful six-penny mechanics —"

Mechanics are manual laborers. They purchased less expensive tickets than nobles.

"Caves" comes from the Latin *caveae*, meaning "seats." The word "wedges" comes from the definition of the Latin *cunei*, meaning "wedge-shaped seat divisions."

"But the better and braver — more splendidly dressed — sort of your people!" Damplay said. "Plush-and-velvet outsides that stick to your house round like so many eminences —"

These expensively dressed playgoers decorated the theater like so many supporting columns as they sat in galleries around the theater. They paid more money for tickets and so supported the theater.

"Of clothes, not understandings?" John Trygust said. "They are at pawn."

A pawn is used as collateral for debt, but in this society, a pawn is also a peacock, whose brilliant feathers are like the expensive clothing of some playgoers.

He continued, "Well, I take these as a part of your people, though."

These expensively dressed playgoers are like Damplay: more splendid in clothing than intelligence.

John Trygust then asked, "What do you bring to me from these people?"

"You have heard, boy, the ancient poets had it in their purpose always to please this people?" Damplay asked.

Probee began, "Aye, their chief aim was —"

Damplay interrupted, "— *populo ut placerent* (if he understands so much)."

He was not certain that John Trygust understood Latin.

John Trygust did understand Latin and he finished the quotation: "— *quas fecissent fabulas.*"

Populo ut placerent quas fecissent fabulas is Latin for "Whatever plays they make should please the people" (Terence, *Andria*, Prologue, 3).

He continued, "I understand that since I learned Terence in the third form at Westminster. Go on, sir."

"Third form" is a junior grade at school.

Probee said, "Now, these people have employed us to you in all their names to ask for an excellent play from you."

"For they have had very mean — inferior — plays from this shop of late, the stage, as you call it," Damplay said.

John Trygust said, "Truly, gentlemen, I have no wares that I dare thrust upon the people with praise. But this, such as it is, I will venture with — risk to have appear before — your people, your gay gallant people, so long as you again will undertake for them that they shall know a good play when they hear it and will have the conscience and ingenuity and nobility of mind and high-mindedness besides to confess it."

The boy wanted Probee and Damplay to guarantee the audience's fairness. He wanted the two men to guarantee that the audience would recognize a good play when they saw it and that they would be fair-minded enough to confess that it was a good play.

Probee replied, "We'll pass our words for that. We'll vouch for it. You shall have a brace — a pair — of us to engage ourselves."

"You'll tender your names, gentlemen, to our book then?" John Trygust said.

This was metaphorically a book in a shop. A person would make a purchase on credit, and the person's name would be written in an account book. Probee and Damplay would stay and see the play: That was their purchase. They would also give their words to fairly evaluate the play.

"Yes, here's Master Probee, a man of most powerful speech and parts to persuade," Damplay said.

"And Master Damplay, who will make good all he undertakes," Probee said.

John Trygust said:

"Good Master Probee and Master Damplay! I like your securities: I trust your assurances.

"Whence do you write yourselves? Where do you come from?"

Probee said, "We are of London; we are gentlemen, but knights' brothers and knights' friends, I assure you."

They were younger brothers. In the tradition of primogeniture, the oldest son would inherit the bulk of the father's estate.

Damplay added, "And we are knights' fellows, too. Every poet writes 'squire' now."

England was and is a class-conscious society. An esquire is a gentleman, and sometimes poets' publishers would add "esquire" to the name of the authors they published, whether or not the author actually had the right to use that title.

Historically, a squire or esquire was a knight's attendant, one who hoped to himself become a knight.

"You are good names!" John Trygust said. "Very good men, both of you! I accept you."

Damplay asked, "And what is the title of your play here? *The Magnetic Lady*?"

"Yes, sir, an attractive title that the author has given it," John Trygust said.

"Attractive" means 1) pleasing, and 2) having magnetic force.

Probee said, "*A magnete*, I warrant you."

He was confirming that the title was attractive, as a magnet is attractive. Such a title would attract an audience.

Damplay said, "Oh, no, from *magnus, magna, magnum*!"

Damplay's Latin was faulty. *Magnus, magna, magnum* is a first and second declension adjective meaning "big" or "great." Probee, however, was not using that adjective. *A magnete* means "from a magnet." *Magnes* is the Latin word for "magnetic" or "magnet." It is mixed (third) declension.

John Trygust pointed to Probee, whose Latin was correct, and said, "This gentleman has found the true magnitude —"

Damplay interrupted, "— of his portal or entry to the work, according to Vitruvius."

Vitruvius was a Roman architect. A portal could be an elaborate entrance to a theater.

John Trygust said:

"Sir, all our work is done without a portal — or Vitruvius. "*In foro*, as a true comedy should be."

This comedic play did not have an elaborate set. *In foro* is Latin for "in an open court or space." Classical comedies also did not have elaborate sets and were *in foro*.

He continued:

"And what is concealed within is brought out and made present by report."

In classical plays, important events that happened offstage would be reported by a messenger or other person. In *The Magnetic Lady*, a dinner party occurs offstage and some of the characters on stage report on the events that happen during it.

"We see that is not always observed by your authors of these times, or scarcely any other," Damplay said.

Modern authors often did not follow the traditions observed by classical playwrights.

Such traditions included the three unities: unity of action, unity of time, and unity of place. Ben Jonson sometimes followed these unities:

The play had one main plot, with no subplots.

The play took place within one day.

The play took place in one main location.

John Trygust said, "Where it is not at all known, how should it be observed? The most of those your people call authors never dreamed of any *decorum* or what was proper in the scene, but grope at it in the dark and feel or fumble for it. I speak it both with their leave and the leave of your people."

"Leave" means "permission."

Yes, many playwrights of Ben Jonson's time didn't know much about stage theory.

Damplay asked, "But why is the play subtitled *Humors Reconciled*, I would like to know?"

By the end of this play, after some major revelations, all the characters will be reconciled to truth. *The Magnetic Lady* is a comedy and has a happy ending.

"I can satisfy you there, too — if you will," John Trygust said. "But perhaps you desire not to be satisfied."

"No?" Damplay asked. "Why should you conceive that to be so, boy?"

John Trygust said:

"My conceit — my understanding — is not ripe yet; I'll tell you that soon."

He was not sure how much to tell Damplay about the play. Often, it is better to simply watch a play without knowing much before seeing it. It is true, however, that a little knowledge can whet the appetite for seeing a play.

John Trygust continued:

"The author, Ben Jonson, beginning his studies of this kind with *Every Man In His Humor* and afterward, *Every Man Out of His Humor*, and since, continuing in all his plays (especially those of the comic thread whereof *The New Inn* was the most recent) some recent humors still, or manners of men, which went along with the times, finding himself now near the close or shutting up of his circle, has fancied to himself in idea and his imagination this magnetic mistress."

Ben Jonson's emblem (heraldic device) had the motto *Deest quod duceret orbem*: That which should complete the circle is lacking.

Ben Jonson, however, saw *The Magnetic Lady* as his last comedy of manners, one that would close the circle of his plays about humors. One more play by Jonson appeared on stage after *The Magnetic Lady* — *A Tale of a Tub* — but that play may be a revision of a play he wrote at or near the beginning of his career.

John Trygust continued:

"A lady, a brave, bountiful housekeeper [keeper of a house, not a housecleaner] and a virtuous widow, who, having a young niece ripe for a man and marriageable, Ben Jonson makes that his center attractive to draw thither a diversity of guests, all persons of different humors to make up his perimeter and circumference. And this he has called *Humors Reconciled*."

The center of Ben Jonson's comedy is the magnetic lady, who is virtuous and attractive and attracts people to her house.

The subtitle of Ben Jonson's comedy is *Humors Reconciled*.

"A bold undertaking!" Probee said. "And far greater than the reconciliation and harmony of both churches — Protestant and Catholic — the quarrel between humors having been much the ancienter and, in my poor opinion, the root of all schism and faction, both in church and commonwealth."

John Trygust said:

"Such is the opinion of many wise men who meet at this shop still, but how Ben Jonson will succeed in this play we cannot tell, and he himself (it seems) less cares.

"For he will not be entreated by us to give it a prologue. He has lost too much time that way — writing prologues — already, he says. He will not woo the gentle, well-born ignorance so much.

"But not worrying or caring about all vulgar — common and ordinary — censure, as not depending on common approbation, he is confident it shall super-please judicious spectators, and to them he leaves it to work with the rest by example or otherwise."

Ben Jonson was confident that his play would greatly appeal to judicious spectators, and he hoped that judicious spectators would be good examples for less judicious spectators to follow.

"He may be deceived in that, boy," Damplay said. "Few follow examples now, especially if the examples are good."

John Trygust said:

"The play is ready to begin, gentlemen, I tell you, lest you might defraud the expectation of the people for whom you are delegates!

"Please take a couple of seats and plant yourselves here as near my standing — where I stand — as you can.

"May everything you see fly to the mark."

In other words: May every satiric arrow hit its target.

John Trygust continued:

"Judge it to be good or bad freely — as long as you don't interrupt the series of dialogue or thread of the plot, to break or pucker and disrupt it with unnecessary questions.

"For I must tell you (not out of my own dictamen and command, but the author's), a good play is like a skein of silk that, if you take it up by the right end, you may wind off at pleasure on the bottom or card of your discourse in a tale or so, how you will."

A bottom is a core that thread is wound around.

A card is a comb with iron teeth used to comb fibers.

John Trygust continued:

"But if you light on the wrong end, you will metaphorically pull all into a knot or elf-lock (tangled hair), which nothing but the shears or a candle will undo or separate."

The knots and tangles must be cut out or burned off.

"Wait!" Damplay said. "Who are these people, I ask you?"

He had seen some actors just offstage. The play was about to start.

John Trygust said, "Because it is your first question, and these are the prime — first and best — persons in the play, it would in civility require an answer. But I have heard the poet affirm that the most unlucky scene in a play is that which needs an interpreter, especially when the auditory are awake, and such are you, he presumes."

Do good plays require interpreters? Ancient plays often had a chorus that commented on the action of the play.

Probee and Damplay are the interpreters of this play; they form a chorus that will comment on the action of this play.

John Trygust concluded:

"Ergo — therefore — pay attention."

Probee and Damplay took their seats and watched the beginning of the play.

CHAPTER 1

— 1.1 —

Compass and Captain Ironside met on the street in front of Lady Loadstone's house. Compass studied mathematics and its application to other sciences, and Captain Ironside was a soldier. They were friends and worthy men. The two men were "brothers," but not in a biological sense.

Lady Loadstone was hosting a dinner, and Compass wanted Captain Ironside to attend the dinner with him.

Compass greeted his friend:

"Welcome, good Captain Ironside, and brother, you shall go along with me. I'm lodged nearby here at a noble lady's house on the street, the Lady Loadstone's. She is one who will bid us welcome.

"At her house there are gentlewomen and male guests of different humors [strong personality characteristics], carriage [social behavior], constitution [disposition], and profession [belief, or occupation], too, but so diametrically opposed one to another and so much opposed that, if I can but hold them all together and draw them to a sufferance and tolerance of each other just until the dissolution — the end — of the dinner, I shall have just occasion to believe my wit is magisterial, and we ourselves shall take infinite delight in the outcome."

A magisterial intelligence is a masterful intelligence. The *magisterium* is the philosopher's stone, which was greatly desired by alchemists. It was thought to be able to turn lead into gold. A magisterial intelligence can turn pen and paper into a literary masterwork.

Compass was looking forward to the dinner. Many different personality types would attend Lady Loadstone's dinner, and there was great potential for arguments to break out. He had a reputation for getting along with many different kinds of people, and he wanted to test his ability to keep the guests at the dinner peaceful. But if he failed and arguments broke out, then that would provide entertainment for his friend Captain Ironside and him. And if at the end all arguments were resolved, that also would be a comedy.

Captain Ironside replied, "Truly, brother Compass, you shall pardon me. I don't love so to multiply the number of my acquaintances when doing so can ruin a meal. It will take away much from my freedom and bind me to follow the most trivial customs of etiquette."

He preferred to eat in peace and quiet and not to engage in the customs of etiquette that required people to get along with and be polite to other people whom they disliked.

Compass said, "Why, Ironside, you know I am a scholar and am in part a soldier; I have been employed by some of the greatest statesmen of the kingdom these many years, and in my time I have conversed with people who had various kinds of humors, suiting myself so to company, with the result that honest men and knaves, goodfellows and revelers, hypocrites, all sorts of people, although never so divided and separated by differences in and among themselves, have labored to agree still in their treatment and handling of me (which has been fair, too)."

In other words: Although all of these people I have met in my life are very different from each other, they have always treated me fairly (as I have treated them).

Captain Ironside said:

"Sir, I confess you to be one well read — knowledgeable — in men and manners, and that usually the most ungoverned and uncontrolled persons, you being present, would rather subject themselves to your censure — your criticism and judgment — than give you the least occasion of distaste and displeasure by making you the target of their jokes."

Captain Ironside agreed that other people, even the most ungoverned, treated Compass well because they respected him. In turn, Compass treated them well.

Captain Ironside continued:

"But — to deal plainly with you, as a brother — whenever I distrust my own valor, I'll never rely upon another's wit and intelligence, or attempt to rescue or save myself by relying on the opinion of your judgment, gravity, discretion, or whatever else."

The *Oxford English Dictionary* has as one meaning of "valor" this: "Worth or importance due to personal qualities or to rank."

The dinner would include people of different social ranks, but even if Captain Ironside were to be of a lower social rank than some or all of the other dinner guests and got in an argument with someone, he would not rely on Compass to smooth things over.

Captain Ironside continued:

"But, if I am absent, you're sure to have less wit-work — that is, less need to use your ingenuity and intelligence — gentle brother, my humor being as stubborn as the rest, and as unmanageable."

Captain Ironside was aware that if he attended the dinner, he could very well get into one or more arguments.

Compass replied, "You mistake my characterization and valuation of your friendship all this while, or at what rate I reckon your assistance, knowing by long experience, to such animals, half-hearted creatures as these are, your fox — your sword — there, unkennelled and unsheathed with a choleric, angry, ghastly aspect, or two or three comminatory — threatening — terms, would make them run in their fears to any hole of shelter, worth a day's laughter. I am for the sport — the entertainment — and for nothing else."

Part of the entertainment would be to see Captain Ironside, if he had need to, frighten cowards who attack him and make them run away. He would use his fox — a type of sword — to do that.

Captain Ironside objected:

"But brother, I have seen a coward, meeting with a man as valiant as our Saint George (not knowing him to be such, or having the least opinion that he was so), set upon him roundly, aye, and swinge — beat — him soundly.

"And in the virtue and strength of that error, having once overcome, resolved forever after to err, and think no person nor no creature more valiant than himself."

Sometimes cowards get lucky in a fight, even when they are fighting a valiant man (and especially when they don't realize the man is valiant).

Compass said:

"I think that, too.

"But, brother, if I could over-entreat you and persuade you to do more than you want to do, I have a little plot against the other dinner guests.

"If you would be contented to endure a sliding, passing reprehension and condemnation and finding of faults at my hands, to hear yourself or your profession glanced at — criticized indirectly — in a few slighting terms, it would beget me such a main — strong — authority on the by (as a result) and do yourself no disrepute at all."

Compass' plot involves him criticizing Captain Ironside and his profession of soldier. This criticism, he says, would benefit him and would have no ill effect on Captain Ironside.

Captain Ironside replied:

"Compass, I know that universal causes in nature produce nothing except as meeting particular causes, to determine those and specify their acts."

Aristotle did not accept Plato's theory of ideal Forms. He did think that common, universal characteristics existed, but only in relation to material examples. Instead of believing in the ideal Form of Tree, Aristotle recognized that many individual trees existed and they shared common, universal characteristics that identified them as being trees.

Captain Ironside continued:

"This is a piece of Oxford science and philosophy that has stayed with me ever since I left that place, and I have often found the truth thereof in my private passions and feelings.

"For I never feel myself perturbed with any general words against my profession of soldiery, unless by some smart stroke upon myself they awake and stir me."

In other words: General condemnations against the military profession did not bother Captain Ironside. What would make him angry was a condemnation made directly against him: an individual soldier.

Captain Ironside continued:

"In addition, to wise and well-experienced men, words carry only superficial meaning. They have no power, except with dull grammarians, whose souls are nothing but a *syntaxis* — arrangement — of them."

A proverb stated, "Words are but wind."

A physical attack on Captain Ironside, however, would be strongly resisted by him.

Seeing someone coming toward them, Compass said:

"Here comes our parson, Parson Palate here, a 'venerable youth'! I must greet him.

"And he's a great clerk and cleric! He's going to the lady's, and, although you see him thus without his cope, I dare assure you, he's our parish pope."

A cope is an outer ecclesiastical garment. Parson Palate was not wearing one.

Parson Palate walked over to them.

Compass said, "May God save my reverend clergyman, Parson Palate!"

"The witty Master Compass!" Parson Palate replied. "How is it with you? How are you?"

Compass replied, "My lady waits for you and for your counsel touching — concerning — her niece, Mistress Placentia Steel, who strikes the fire of fully fourteen years old today, ripe for a husband."

Flint striking steel creates a spark that can light a fire.

The fire she is experiencing is metaphorical: Placentia Steel has reached puberty and is feeling sexual fire.

In this society, fourteen was a young age for a bride.

Parson Palate said:

"Aye, she chimes, she chimes."

The chimes, as of a bell ringing the time, announce that she's ready and ripe enough to be married. She rings out her sexual desirability.

He continued:

"Have you seen the Doctor Rut, the house physician? He's sent for, too."

"Sent for to counsel her?" Compass said. "It's time you were there. Make haste and give it a round, brisk, quick dispatch, so that we may go to dinner in good time, parson, and drink a health or two more to the business."

Parson Palate exited.

Captain Ironside said, "This is a strange put-off!"

He felt that Compass had been rude to Parson Palate in how he had sent him on his way.

Captain Ironside continued:

"He is a reverend youth, and you treat him very surreverently — not reverently — I think.

"What do you call him? Palate Please? Or Parson Palate?"

Compass said:

"All's one, but shorter."

Indeed, "Palate Please" is one syllable shorter than "Parson Palate." Both together mean that he is a parson who pleases his palate.

Compass continued:

"I can give you a description of his character."

Compass then described the parson's character, in couplets:

"He is the prelate of the parish here

"And governs all the dames, appoints the cheer [food and entertainment],

"Writes down the bills of fare, pricks [records] all the guests,

"Makes all the matches and the marriage feasts

"Within the ward, draws up all the parish wills,

"Designs [Arranges] the legacies, and strokes the gills

"Of the chief mourners."

Tickling the gills of trout was a way of catching them. Metaphorically, Parson Palate flatters the chief mourners as a preparation for taking money from them.

Compass continued:

"And, whoever lacks

"Of all the kindred, he has first his blacks [black hangings for funerals]."

Parson Palate probably rents out the black hangings as a source of income.

The "whoever lacks" is ambiguous. It can refer to 1) a lack of money, or 2) a lack of a family member due to death.

Compass continued:

"Thus holds he weddings up, and burials,

"As his main tithing [source of income], with the gossips' stalls,

"Their pews."

Parson Palate makes money by renting pews to godparents, aka gossips.

Compass continued:

"He's top still [always] at the public mess [always sits at the head of the table],

"Comforts the widow and the fatherless

"In funeral sack [sackcloth], sits above the alderman,

"For of the wardmote quest [a town ward's judicial inquiry] he better can [knows]

"The mystery than the Levitic law."

"That piece of clerkship [scholarship] does his vestry awe."

Parson Palate understood secular law better than he understood church law. Many parsons attempted to understand such mysteries as the Trinity, but Parson Palate worked to understand secular mysteries. The people in his congregation were awed by his knowledge of secular law.

Compass continued:

"He is as he conceives himself, a fine,

"Well-furnished and apparellèd divine."

Parson Palate concerned himself much with his income, and he knew much about secular matters. He also had a high opinion of himself and was very well dressed.

Different kinds of 'fine" exist. A person can have a fine figure or a fine mind.

Different kinds of "well-furnished" exist. The phrase can refer to a house that has fine furniture or to a well-stocked mind.

Actor/writer/director/raconteur Peter Ustinov was once asked why he read so many books. He replied that since he was a prisoner of his mind, he wanted it to be well furnished.

The description of Parson Palate was an epigram: a short witty poem.

"Who made this epigram?" Captain Ironside asked. "You?"

"No, the one who made it is as great clerk — scholar — as any is of his bulk," Compass said. "Ben Jonson made it."

This is true: Ben Jonson wrote *The Magnetic Lady*.

Ben Jonson was a bulky — heavy — man. At one time, he was just short of 20 stone, or 280 pounds. According to Jonson, he had a "mountain belly."

Jonson's knowledge of literature, including classical literature, was impressive: It was weighty.

"But what is the character description of Doctor Rut?" Captain Ironside asked.

Compass replied:

"The same man — Ben Jonson — made both character descriptions, but the description of Doctor Rut is shorter, and not in rhymed couplets, but unrhymed blank verse.

"I'll tell you that, too.

"Rut is a young physician to the family, who, letting God alone, ascribes to nature more than her share."

In a religious age, he ignored God and God's help in healing.

Compass continued:

"He is licentious in discourse."

In other words: He says more than he should.

Compass continued:

"And in his life he is a self-confessed voluptuary and lewd sexualist.

"He is the slave of money, a low buffoon and cruel fool in manners.

"He is obscene and indecorous in language, which he vents and speaks for wit.

"He is saucy and insolent in his logics and disputing.

"He is anything but civil or a man."

Seeing people approaching them, Compass said, "Look, here they are!"

Lady Loadstone, Parson Palate, and Doctor Rut entered the scene.

Compass said to Captain Ironside:

"And they are walking with My Lady in consultation before the door.

"We will slip in as if we didn't see them."

Compass and Captain Ironside exited the scene and entered Lady Loadstone's house, where Compass resided.

Lady Loadstone, Parson Palate, and Doctor Rut talked about Placentia Steel, Lady Loadstone's niece. Today was her fourteenth birthday, and Lady Loadstone believed that she was ready to be married.

"Aye, it is his fault that my niece, Placentia, is not bestowed and given in marriage," Lady Loadstone said. "It is my brother Interest's fault."

"Who, old Sir Moth?" Parson Palate asked.

"He keeps off all her suitors, keeps her marriage portion still in his hands, and will not part with it on any terms," Lady Loadstone said.

The marriage portion was Placentia's dowry. Sir Interest Moth had control of the money until Placentia was married.

Mathew 6:19-20 (King James Version) states:

"19: *Lay not up for yourselves treasures upon earth, where moth and rust doth corrupt, and where thieves break through and steal:*

"20: *But lay up for yourselves treasures in heaven, where neither moth nor rust doth corrupt, and where thieves do not break through nor steal:*"

Sir Interest Moth, however, was a usurer, and he was busy laying up for himself treasure on earth.

"*Hinc illae lachrimae*," Parson Palate said. "Thus flows the cause of the main grievance."

Hinc illae lachrimae is Latin for "Hence [come] these tears."

The line is a quotation from Terence, *Andria*, line 126.

"That — the grievance — it is a main one," Doctor Rut said. "How much is the marriage portion?"

"No petty sum," Lady Loadstone said.

"No more or less than sixteen thousand pounds," Parson Palate said.

"He should be forced, madam, to lay it down and release it," Doctor Rut said. "When is it payable?"

"When she is married," Lady Palate said.

"Marry her, marry her, madam," Parson Palate said.

"Get her married," Doctor Rut said. "Lose not a day, an hour —"

Parson Palate interrupted:

"— not a minute. Pursue your project real."

"Real" can mean 1) genuine, actual, 2) real estate, real property, and/or 3) chattel real — a lease or ward.

Placentia Steel is a ward of Lady Loadstone.

Hmm. Fourteen is a young age to be married. The haste for Placentia Steel to be married may have much to do with getting sixteen thousand pounds out of the hands of Sir Moth Interest, the brother of Lady Loadstone. But there could be a different, additional reason.

Parson Palate continued:

"Master Compass advised you, too. He is the perfect instrument your Ladyship should sail by."

Parson Palate respected Compass.

Doctor Rut said, "Now, Master Compass is a fine, witty man. I saw him go in just now."

"Has he gone in?" Lady Loadstone asked.

"Yes, and a feather with him," Parson Palate said. "He seems to be a soldier."

Captain Ironside was wearing a feather in his hat. At the time, that was a mark of a military man.

"He is some new suitor, madam," Doctor Rut said.

"I am beholden to Compass," Lady Loadstone said. "He always brings a variety of good persons to my table, and I must thank him, although my brother Interest dislikes and disapproves of it a little."

"Sir Moth Interest likes nothing that runs your way," Parson Palate said. "If you like something, he doesn't like it."

"Truly, and the other — Compass — doesn't care about Sir Moth Interest's opinion," Doctor Rut said. "Compass will go his own way, if he thinks it right."

Lady Loadstone said:

"Compass is a true friend.

"And there's Master Practice, the fine young man of law who comes to the house. My brother does not tolerate him because he thinks that Master Practice is by me assigned for — intended to marry — my niece.

"My brother will not hear of it."

Doctor Rut said:

"Not of that ear."

"To hear of both ears" means to be impartial and to hear both sides of an argument. In this case, Sir Moth Interest is metaphorically deaf in one ear and will not hear the argument that Placentia ought to marry the lawyer Master Practice.

Doctor Rut continued:

"But yet Your Ladyship does wisely in it —"

Parson Palate interrupted:

"— it will make him to lay down the marriage portion sooner, if he but dreams you'll match her with a lawyer."

A lawyer would know how to get the dowry money from Sir Moth Interest.

"So Master Compass says," Lady Loadstone said. "It is between the lawyer and the courtier who shall have and marry Placentia."

"Who, Sir Diaphanous Silkworm?" Parson Palate asked.

Yes, Sir Diaphanous Silkworm was the courtier.

"A fine gentleman," Doctor Rut said. "He is Old Master Silkworm's heir."

Parson Palate said, "And he is a neat, well-dressed courtier, of a most elegant thread — appearance and clothing."

"And so my gossip — my companion — Polish assures me," Lady Loadstone said. "Here she comes!"

Mistress Polish entered the scene.

Lady Loadstone said, "Good Polish, you are welcome, truly! How are thou, gentle Polish?"

"Who's this?" Doctor Rut whispered to Parson Palate.

Parson Palate quietly answered, "She is Dame Polish, the she-parasite of Lady Loadstone. She is her much-talking, soothing and flattering, sometime governing gossip."

A she-parasite is a female dependent.

A gossip is a friend or companion.

Mistress Polish had been Placentia's guardian.

Madame Polish said, "Your Ladyship is still the Lady Loadstone who draws and draws to you guests of all sorts: the courtiers, the soldiers, the scholars, the travelers, physicians, and divines, as Doctor Ridley wrote, and Doctor Barlow! They both have written about you and Master Compass."

Mark Ridley wrote *The Navigators Supply* (1597), and William Barlow wrote *Magneticall Advertisements ... experiments concerning the nature and properties of the Load-stone* (1616).

"We intend that they shall write more before long," Lady Loadstone said.

Mistress Polish said:

"Alas, they are both dead, if it please you."

"If it please you" means "I hope you don't mind my saying so."

Mark Ridley had died in 1624, and William Barlow had died in 1625.

Mistress Polish continued:

"But Your Ladyship means well, and shall mean well, so long as I live.

"How does your fine niece, my charge, Mistress Placentia Steel? How is she?"

A "charge" is a responsibility.

Mistress Polish helped take care of her charge: Placentia Steel.

"She is not well," Lady Loadstone said.

"Not well?" Mistress Polish asked.

"Her doctor says so," Lady Loadstone said.

Doctor Rut said:

"She is not very well.

"She cannot shoot arrows at butts [targets] and practice archery, or manage and ride a great warhorse, but she can crunch a sack of small coal-cinder, eat limestone and hair, soap-ashes [wood ashes used in making soap], loam, and she has a dainty, delicate, delightful spice — perfume — of the green sickness."

The green sickness is anemia brought about by puberty in young women and causing a faint greenish complexion. Some of the odd "snacks" listed here may replace iron lost through menstruation. An unusual appetite for odd items is a sign of anemia due to iron deficiency — and it is a sign of pregnancy.

This society believed that green sickness afflicted virgins, and one cure was to marry the young woman to a man.

Sir Moth Interest was willing for Placentia to continue to be sick and not marry because he would keep control of her money.

Now that Placentia was a young woman, she was giving up male exercises such as target shooting and riding large horses. She was no longer a tomboy.

"'Od shield!" Mistress Polish said.

This means, "God shield and protect us!"

Doctor Rut then said:

"Or she has a dainty, delicate, delightful spice — perfume — of the dropsy."

Dropsy is edema, which causes swelling, including a bloated stomach.

He continued:

"The illness is a toy, a trifle, a thing of nothing.

"But My Lady here, her noble aunt —"

Mistress Polish said, "She is a noble aunt, and a right worshipful — distinguished and worthy of respect — lady, and a virtuous one, I know it well."

Doctor Rut said, "Well, if you know it, peace — be quiet."

"Good sister Polish, hear your betters speak," Parson Palate said.

Mistress Polish said:

"Sir, I will speak, with My good Lady's leave, and speak and speak again.

"I did bring up My Lady's niece, Mistress Placentia Steel, with my own daughter, who's Placentia, too, and waits upon My Lady as her serving-woman."

"Placentia" means "pleasure." So does "Pleasance," which is the name of Mistress Polish's daughter. So both have the same name: Pleasure.

Mistress Polish continued:

"Her Ladyship well knows Mistress Placentia Steel, as I said, her curious — fastidious and discriminating — niece, was left a legacy to me — bequeathed to me — by father and mother, along with the nurse, Keep, who tended her."

In other words, Mistress Polish became Placentia's guardian.

Mistress Polish continued:

"Her mother died in childbed of complications resulting from her birth, and her father lived for not long afterward because he loved her mother.

"They were a godly couple!

"Yet both died, as must we all. No creature is immortal, I have heard our pastor say, no, not even the faithful, and they did die, as I said, both in one month —"

The first part of Psalm 89:48 states, "*What man is he that liveth, and shall not see death?*" (King James Version).

Doctor Rut whispered to Parson Palate, "Surely Mistress Polish is not likely to be long-lived, if she expends and wastes her breath like this."

Mistress Polish continued:

"And did bequeath her to my care and hand to polish and bring up."

The polish would be acquired through education and training.

Mistress Polish continued:

"I molded her and fashioned her and formed her; she had the sweat both of my brows and brains, My Lady knows it, since she could write a quarter old."

The words "since she could write a quarter old" mean "since she — Pleasance — was a week old."

The word "quarter" means "a fourth of a lunar month."

Pleasance's mother died giving birth to her, and her father quickly died afterward in the same month, and so Pleasance became Mistress Polish's ward when Pleasance was one fourth of a lunar month old — one week old.

One meaning of "write" is "to be age [such-and-such]."

To tease Mistress Polish, Lady Loadstone interpreted "write" in the sense of "writing letters and words":

"I don't know that she could write so early, my good gossip.

"But I do know that she was so long in your care until she was twelve years old. It was then that I called for her and took her home, for which I thank you, Polish, and I am beholden to you."

Doctor Rut whispered to Parson Palate, "I for sure thought that she had a lease of talking for nine lives —"

A lease is a legal arrangement. Some leases can be for a lifetime, but some were for more than one lifetime so the lease would apply to descendants. But if Mistress Polish were like a cat and had nine lives, she would be talking throughout each of them.

Parson Palate interrupted, "— it may be she has."

Overhearing him, Mistress Polish said to Parson Palate:

"Sir, sixteen thousand pounds was then her portion, for she was indeed their only child. And this was to be paid upon her marriage, provided that she married still — consistent — with My good Lady's liking here, her aunt.

"I heard the will read: Master Steel, her father, the world condemned him to be very rich and very hard, and he did stand condemned with that vain world until, as it was proved afterward, he left almost as much more to good uses in Sir Moth Interest's hands, the hands of My Lady's brother, whose sister Master Steel had married.

"Sir Moth Interest holds all the money in his close grip."

Master Steel had married the sister of Lady Loadstone and Sir Moth Interest. Sir Moth was now the trustee of Master Steel's estate, including the money that was supposed to go to charity and the money that was supposed to be Placentia's dowry.

Master Steel had left almost sixteen thousand pounds to good uses — charity. But since Sir Moth Interest was taking care of the money, and since as a usurer he considered earning interest to be a good use of money, he was probably using the money in usury.

Mistress Polish continued:

"But Master Steel was liberal and generous, and he was a fine man, and his wife was a dainty dame, and she was a religious, and a bountiful —"

Compass and Captain Ironside now stepped forward.

They had entered somewhat earlier and had listened to the conversation, but now they walked over to the others.

"You knew her, Master Compass?" Mistress Polish asked.

"Her" was Master Steel's wife, the mother of Placentia.

"Spare the torture," Compass said. "I do confess without it."

Some prisoners were tortured to exact confessions.

Compass was tortured by hearing about Master Steel's wife because it reminded him that she was now dead. He had respected her.

"And her husband?" Mistress Polish asked. "What a fine couple they were, and how they lived?"

"Yes," Compass said.

"And loved together like a pair of turtledoves?" Mistress Polish asked.

Turtledoves are symbols of constancy in love — they are lovebirds.

"Yes," Compass said.

"And feasted all the neighbors?" Mistress Polish asked.

"Take her away," Compass said. "Somebody who has mercy —"

Doctor Rut whispered to Parson Palate, "Oh, he knows Mistress Steel, it seems!"

Compass continued:

"— or any measure of compassion.

"Doctors, if you are Christians, undertake responsibility — one for the soul, the other for the body!"

The doctors were Parson Palate, Doctor of Theology, and Doctor Rut, Doctor of Medicine.

Mistress Polish said, "Mistress Steel would dispute and debate with the Doctors of Divinity at her own table! And the Spital preachers! And find out the errors of the Armenians."

Preachers spoke Spital Sermons at the Church of St. Mary Spitalfields, which was near the hospital of St. Mary.

Doctor Rut asked, "Do you mean the Arminians?"

Doctor Rut was right. She actually meant the followers of James Arminius, aka Jacobus Arminius, who proposed that God's sovereignty and human free will are compatible. This was a reaction to the Calvinist belief of predestination: that God chose which human beings he wanted to save; even before they were born, all human beings were predestined either for Heaven or for Hell.

The Arminians can be seen as a middle way between Calvinism and Catholicism.

"I say the Armenians," Madam Polish said.

"I say so, too!" Compass said.

He wanted to have some fun at her expense.

"So Master Polish called them, the Armenians!' Mistress Polish said.

"And the Medes and the Persians, didn't he?" Compass said.

Compass was having fun with her, hoping that she would adopt these malapropisms. And so she did, using "Medes" to refer to those people who were middling — lukewarm — when it came to religious observance. She also used "Persians" to mean Precisians: strict Puritans.

Mistress Polish rose to his expectations:

"Yes, he knew them, and so did Mistress Steel! She was his pupil.

"The Armenians, he would say, were worse than Papists!

"And then the Persians were our Puritans, and they had the fine piercing wits!"

"And who were the Medes?" Compass asked.

"The middlemen, the lukewarm Protestants!" Mistress Polish said.

"Out, out! Bah, bah!" Doctor Rut said. "That's what I say to the middle way!"

"Sir, she would find them by their branching: their branching sleeves, branched cassocks, and branched doctrine, beside their texts," Mistress Polish said.

"Branching" and "branched" usually refer to embroidery, but when Mistress Polish refers to "branching doctrine," she means "branching away from true religion," aka "causing a schism or heresy."

"Stint, carline!" Doctor Rut said. "Stop, old woman! I'll not listen to her. Confute her, parson."

A "carline" is an old woman.

"I respect no persons, chaplains, or doctors. I will speak," Mistress Polish said.

By "persons," Mistress Polish meant "parsons."

"Yes," Lady Loadstone said. "As long as she speaks reason, let her."

Doctor Rut said, "Death, she cannot speak reason."

"Death" is an oath: "By God's death."

"Nor can she speak sense, if we are masters of our senses," Compass said.

Captain Ironside said, "What madwoman have they got here to bait — to torment?"

An entertainment of the time was bear-baiting, an activity in which dogs tormented a bear that was tied to a stake.

Another entertainment: Some people visited mentally ill people and laughed at them.

Mistress Polish said, "Sir, I am mad in truth and to the purpose, and I cannot but be mad, to hear My Lady's dead sister slighted, witty Mistress Steel!"

Chances are, Her Lady's dead sister was not slighted, just Mistress Polish's interpretation of what Her Lady's sister believed.

Captain Ironside said, "If she had a wit, death has gone near to spoil it, assure yourself."

In other words: Death has destroyed her good intelligence.

Mistress Polish said:

"She was both witty [intelligent] and zealous in her faith, and she lighted all the tinder of the truth — she inspired fervor — (as one said) of religion in our parish.

"She was too learnèd to live long with us!

"She could — she conned and knew — the Bible in the holy tongue, Hebrew, and read it without pricks."

To read Hebrew without pricks means to read it without torment: to read it fluently.

Also, "pricks" can refer to marks on Hebrew vowels. To read Hebrew without those linguistic marks would be difficult.

Mistress Polish continued:

"She had all her *Masoreth*; she knew Burton and his *Bull*, and scribe Prynne, gent., presto-begone, and all the Pharisees!"

Masoreth is a learnéd edition of the Talmud: a compilation of Jewish civil and ceremonial law and legend.

Henry Burton published *The Baiting of the Popes Bull* in 1627.

William Prynne was a militant Puritan who made attacks in his writings upon church policy under the Archbishop of Canterbury: William Laud. Because of his work *Histriomastix*, in which he criticized theater, he was accused of criticizing the Queen of England, who had performed in a play. The Queen was Henrietta Maria of France, who was married to King Charles I of England. As a result, Prynne spent time in the pillory, and suffered the amputation of both of his ears. Mistress Polish perhaps calls him "gent." instead of "gentleman" because anyone who attacks and criticizes the Queen is not a gentleman. Some of his works list as the author "William Prynne, gent. Lincolnshire."

John Presto was a Protestant divine. The word "prestidigitation" refers to entertaining magic tricks.

"Presto-begone," however, may also or instead refer to Prester John, a legendary Christian priest-king.

Jesus criticized Pharisees for their public performances of piety.

Lady Loadstone said, "Dear gossip, leave at this time, too, and vouchsafe — condescend — to see your charge: my niece."

"I shall obey, if Your wise Ladyship thinks fit," Mistress Polish said. "I know enough to yield to my superiors."

She exited.

Lady Loadstone said:

"She is a good woman!

"But when Mistress Polish is impertinent and grows earnest and strident, a little troublesome and out of season, then her love and zeal transport her."

One meaning of "transport" is "to move from this world to the next world." Another meaning is "to be carried away by emotions."

Compass said:

"I am glad that anything could port — carry — her away from here. We now have hope of dinner, after her long grace."

A long grace is a long prayer before a meal.

Compass continued:

"I have brought Your Ladyship a hungry guest here, a soldier and my brother, Captain Ironside, who being by custom and habit grown a sanguinary — someone who loves to shed the blood of others, the solemn and adopted son of slaughter — is more delighted in the chase of an enemy, an execution (in more ways than one) of three days and nights, than he is delighted by all the hope of numerous succession or happiness of issue — many children — could bring to him —"

In other words, Captain Ironside preferred the act of killing to the act that might result in the production of children.

Doctor Rut whispered to Parson Palate, "He is no suitor to Placentia, then?"

Parson Palate whispered back, "So it would seem."

Compass continued:

"And, if he can get pardon at heaven's hand for all his murders, is in as good case as a new-christened infant, his employments continued to him without interruption, and not allowing him either time or place to commit any other sins but those."

In other words: Captain Ironside has been so busy killing people that he has not been able to commit any other sins such as fornication. If heaven pardons his many killings, then he is as innocent as a newly christened infant.

Compass continued:

"Please make him welcome for a meal, madam."

Lady Loadstone said, "The nobleness of his profession makes his welcome perfect, although your coarse description would seem to sully it."

Of course, Compass had previously gotten his friend's permission to somewhat denigrate his military profession.

Captain Ironside said, "Never, where a beam of so much favor does illustrate and illuminate it, right knowing lady."

Lady Loadstone had looked approvingly at him as if she knew that he was a good man despite just meeting him.

Parson Palate whispered to Doctor Rut, "She has cured — healed — all well."

Lady Loadstone was a peacemaker.

Doctor Rut whispered back, "And Captain Ironside has fitted well the compliment."

He had made a good first impression.

Sir Diaphanous Silkworm and Master Practice entered the scene. Sir Diaphanous Silkworm was a courier, and Master Practice was a lawyer. Both were considered suitable suitors for Placentia.

Compass said:

"Here they come! The prime magnetic guests our Lady Loadstone so respects: the Arctic and the Antarctic!"

Sir Diaphanous Silkworm and Master Practice were the most likely male guests to attract other guests. They were the Arctic and the Antarctic: the places where the Earth's magnetic poles were located.

They were also the two most likely suitors to wed Placentia.

Compass continued:

"Sir Diaphanous Silkworm, a courtier extraordinary who, by diet of meats and drinks, his temperate exercise, choice music, frequent baths, his horary shifts — hourly changes — of shirts and waistcoats, means to immortalize mortality itself, and makes the essence of his whole happiness the trim — fashionable dress — of court!"

"To immortalize mortality" means "to live a very long life."

"I thank you, Master Compass, for your short encomiastic," Sir Diaphanous Silkworm said.

By "encomiastic," he meant "commendation."

"It is much in little, sir," Doctor Rut said.

Compass had described the courtier briefly, but well.

Parson Palate said, "It is concise and quick and lively: the true style of an orator."

Compass said:

"But Master Practice here, My Lady's lawyer, or man of law (for that's the true writing): He is a man so dedicated to his profession and the preferments — promotions and privileges — that go along with it, as scarcely the thundering bruit and uproar of an invasion, another fifteen eighty-eight threatening his country with ruin, would no more work upon and affect him than Syracuse's sack on Archimedes.

"So much he loves that nightcap (lawyer's cap), the bench-gown (lawyer's formal gown that was worn in court) with the broad guard (ornamental trimming] on the back."

The year 1588 was the year the Spanish Armada threatened England but was defeated.

Archimedes of Syracuse, Sicily, a famous mathematician and scientist, devised defensive war machines to protect his city; he was killed in 212 B.C.E. by a Roman soldier when Syracuse was sacked. According to legend, Archimedes was engrossed in solving a mathematical problem and so did not notice the Roman soldier.

Compass continued:

"These show a man betrothed — engaged — to the study of our laws!"

Master Practice replied, "You just think that the practice of law is the crafty impositions of subtle clerks, feats of fine understanding to abuse clots (fools) and clowns (more fools) with, Master Compass, having no ground in nature to sustain it or light from those clear causes that to the inquiry and search of which your mathematical head has so devowed and devoted itself."

Master Practice believed that Compass thought that law lacked the firm foundation and clarity of mathematics, the subject that Compass studied. Law was not mathematical and was not scientific.

Compass replied:

"Tut, all men are philosophers to their inches — to the best of their abilities.

"There inside Lady Loadstone's house is Sir Interest, as able a philosopher in buying and selling, who has reduced his thrift to certain principles, and in that method, as he will tell you instantly, by logarithms, the utmost profit of a stock (investment) employed, be the commodity (what is traded) what it will, the place or time but causing very, very little, or, I may say, no parallax (alteration) at all, in his pecuniary observations!

"He has brought your niece's marriage portion with him, madam; at least, he has brought the man who must receive it."

Compass had referred to Sir Interest, which is an incorrect way to refer to a knight. Sir Moth and Sir Moth Interest are both correct, but not Sir Interest. Such a wrong use of the name indicated Compass' lack of respect for this man.

Compass noticed Sir Moth Interest and Master Bias entering the scene and said:

"Here they come, negotiating the affair.

"You may perceive the contract in their faces and read the indenture.

"If you'd sign them, so be it."

An indenture was a contract that was divided into two halves with serrated edges. One half was given to each of the two people who had made the contract.

Compass believed that Sir Moth Interest and Master Bias were motivated mainly by the making of money. Because of that, Lady Loadstone ought to be careful about accepting their idea about whom Placentia ought to marry.

Their idea was that Placentia ought to marry Master Bias.

Sir Moth Interest and Master Bias walked over to them.

Sir Moth Interest was a usurer, or money-bawd, and brother to Lady Loadstone.

Master Bias was a vi-politic — a vice-politician, aka assistant to an official. The official was Lord Whach'um: Lord What-You-Call-Him.

Parson Palate asked Compass quietly about Master Bias: "What and who is he, Master Compass?"

Compass answered, "He is a vi-politic, or a sub-aiding (aiding-behind-the-scenes) instrument of state: a kind of laborious, painstaking secretary, one who does all the work, to a great man — and is likely to come on and be successful! He is full of attendance and assiduous service, and of such a stride — so confident — in business, political or economic, that his lord may as well stoop to take advice from him and be told what to do and be directed by him in affairs of highest consequence, when he is dulled or wearied with the less!"

Sir Diaphanous Silkworm the courtier said, "He is Master Bias, Lord Whach'um's politic."

A vi-politician can engage in political manipulation. Master Bias probably did some of Lord Whach'um's dirty work for him.

"You know the man?" Compass asked.

Sir Diaphanous Silkworm answered, "I have seen him wait at court there with his maniples — bundles — of papers and petitions."

Master Practice the lawyer said:

"He is a man who overrules others, though, by his authority of living there, and he cares for no man else."

Much of his authority came from his living at court.

Master Practice continued:

"He neglects the sacred letter of the law, and he holds it all to be just a dead heap of civil institutions. It is the rest — the resort, the prop — only of common men and their causes, a farrago, aka hodgepodge, aka confused mass, or a made-dish — something concocted from many ingredients — in court, a thing of nothing."

"And that's your quarrel at him?" Compass said. "A just plea."

Sir Moth Interest said to his sister, Lady Loadstone, "I tell you, sister Loadstone —"

Compass whispered to Captain Ironside, "Hang your ears this way and hear his praises: Now Moth opens."

Master Practice had given a negative view of Master Bias, and now Sir Moth Interest will give a positive view of Master Bias.

Sir Moth Interest said:

"I have brought you here the very man, the jewel of all the court, close-mouthed and secret Master Bias."

Personal secretaries know their superiors' secrets, and so being secretive and close-mouthed can be a good quality in a secretary.

Sir Moth Interest continued:

"Sister, apply him to your side, or you may wear him here on your breast, or hang him in your ear."

Sir Moth Interest called Master Bias a metaphorical jewel:

"He's a fit pendant for a lady's tip — earlobe. He is chrysolite, a gem, the very agate of state and polity. He is cut from the quarry of Machiavelli, as true a cornelian as Tacitus himself, and to be made the brooch to any true state-cap in Europe!"

In other words: He would be an ornament to any politician he assisted. He would help that politician to become more powerful and influential.

According to the *Oxford English Dictionary*, one meaning of "politician" is "A schemer or plotter; a shrewd, sagacious, or crafty person."

Machiavelli, who wrote *The Prince*, had the reputation of being a consummate political manipulator.

Cornelius Tacitus was a Roman historian.

A cornelian is a gemstone, as is a chrysolite and an agate.

Lady Loadstone said, "You praise him, brother, as if you had hope to sell him."

Compass said, "No, madam, as if he had hope to sell — praise — your niece to him."

"Beware your true jests, Master Compass," Lady Loadstone said. "They will not relish or please."

A proverb states, "There's many a true word spoken in jest."

Sir Moth Interest said:

"I will tell you, sister, that I cannot cry his caract — character and carat — up enough: He is unvaluable."

He meant invaluable: very valuable. "Unvaluable" means 1) very valuable, 2) incalculable, and/or 3) worthless.

Some things, of course, that are valuable in some ways can be worthless in other ways — such as being morally bankrupt.

Sir Moth Interest continued:

"All the lords have him in that esteem for his relations [accounts, narratives of events], courants [express messengers], advice, correspondences and letters with this ambassador and that agent. He will insinuate himself into a statist's confidence and find out the secret of that statist —"

A statist is a skilled politician.

Compass said, "— as easy as some cobbler worms a dog."

In this society, a preventative procedure against rabies was to remove a ligament from under a dog's tongue. This was called "worming" the dog.

Sir Moth Interest continued, "— and lock it in the cabinet of his memory —"

Compass said, "— until it turns into a politic insect or a fly thus long."

"It" refers to Master Bias' memory and to Master Bias himself. Master Bias will keep the secret until it becomes politically expedient to reveal it.

Master Bias is a politic insect or fly: something despicable and annoying such as a buzzing fly or other insect.

Sir Moth Interest said, "You may be merry, Master Compass, but although you have the reversion of an office, you are not in it, sir."

Having the reversion of an office meant having the right to succeed in — being next in line to have — it. Eventually, Compass would have that office.

"Remember that," Master Bias said.

This was a threat. Someone like Master Bias knew ways to have someone else get that reversion.

Compass said, "Why, should that frighten me, Master Bi-, from telling whose -ass you are?"

Compass had separated the two syllables of Bias' name so he could call him an ass. Actually, he called him twice-an-ass: a bi-ass.

Sir Moth Interest said, "Sir, he's one who can do his turns there and deliver, too, his letters as punctually and in as good a fashion as ever a secretary can in court."

In other words: Master Bias knew the tricks of the trade of political trickery.

Captain Ironside said, "Why, is it any matter in what fashion a man delivers his letters, as long as he does not open them?"

Master Bias said, "Yes, we have certain precedents in court from which we never swerve once in an age, and, whatsoever Compass thinks, I know the arts and sciences do not directlier — more directly — make a graduate in our universities than a habitual gravity prefers a man in court."

Projecting an aura of gravitas helped a man earn promotions at court. It does that more directly and effectively than having a good education. Sometimes, appearance is more profitable than reality.

Compass said, "Which, by the truer style, some call a formal, flat servility."

A "truer style" is a truer title or name.

"Formal" means "outward." It is an outward appearance of gravitas that may not match what is inside the vi-politician. Some politicians and vi-politicians are hypocritical.

Master Bias said:

"Sir, you may call it what you please. But we who tread the path of public businesses know what a tacit shrug is, or a shrink, the wearing the calotte, the politic hood, and twenty other *parerga*, besides, you secular laymen — you non-political men — don't understand."

In politics, people know how to shrink and show fear when needed. They know who wears the calotte: a sergeant-at-law's hat.

They also know many other things: *Parerga* means "secondary features."

Master Bias said to himself:

"I shall trick Compass, if his reversion should come in my lord's way."

He would find a way to make Compass' reversion the reversion of the politician he served.

"What is that, Master Practice?" Sir Diaphanous Silkworm asked. "You surely know Master Compass' reversion?"

Master Practice said:

"It is a fine place, a fine office: Surveyor of the Projects General.

"I wish I had it."

The office granted monopolies.

"What is it worth?" Parson Palate asked.

"Oh, sir, it is worth a *nemo scit*," Master Practice said.

Nemo scit is Latin for "No one knows," but no doubt one could guess its worth.

Lady Loadstone said to Sir Moth Interest, "We'll think about it before dinner."

She would think about whether Master Bias would be an appropriate suitor for Placentia.

— CHORUS 1 —

John Trygust asked Probee and Damplay, "Now, gentlemen, what censure — judge — you about our *protasis*, or first act? What do you think about it?"

"Well, boy, it is a fair presentment of and performance by your actors," Probee said. "And it is a handsome promise of something to come hereafter."

"But there is nothing done in it, or concluded," Damplay said. "Therefore I say, it is no act."

John Trygust said:

"A fine piece of logic!

"Do you look, Master Damplay, for conclusions in a *protasis*? I thought the law of comedy had reserved them to the *catastrophe*, and that the *epitasis*, as we are taught, and the *catastasis* had been intervening parts, to have been expected. But you would have all come together, it seems. The clock should strike five at once with the acts."

In other words: If all the parts of a play occurred at the same time, the play would be over quickly.

Also in other words: The introduction (*protasis*) of a play is for introducing things; the conclusion (*catastrophe*) of a play is for concluding things.

In classical drama, plays can be divided into four parts:

Protasis: The introductory part of a play, setting forth the characters and the subject of the play. In Jonson's play and many other plays, this is the first act.

Epitasis: Trials and tribulations ensue and build toward a climax. In Jonson's play, the *epitasis* includes negotiations about who will marry Placentia. The number of suitors increases, and the negotiations become complicated.

Catastasis: The action that was initiated in the *epitasis* continues, often resulting in the climax of a drama. The climax can be the turning point and/or a point of highest tension. In 4.4, Compass makes an important discovery.

Catastrophe: The conclusion, which in comedies is happy. In comedies, the *catastrophe* often includes one or more marriages.

Jonson's play has an additional part:

Prologue/Induction: An opening that gives context and gives background details. In Jonson's play, this is the Induction (Introduction) or Chorus.

"Why, if it could do so, it would be well, boy," Damplay said.

John Trygust replied, "Yes, if the nature of a clock were to speak, not strike. So, if a child could be born in a play, and grow up to a man in the first scene, before he went off the stage, and then afterward to come forth a squire and be made a knight, and that knight to travel between the acts and do wonders in the Holy Land, or elsewhere: kill paynims [pagans], wild boars, dun [dull brown] cows, and other monsters; beget himself a reputation and marry an emperor's daughter for his mistress; convert her father's country; and at last come home, lame and all-to-beladen — heavily loaded — with miracles."

Damplay said, "These miracles would please, I assure you, and take — captivate — the people. For there are those of the people who will expect miracles and more than miracles from this pen."

"Do they think this pen — Ben Jonson — can juggle?" John Trygust asked. "I wish we had Hocus-Pocus for them, then, your people, or Travitanto Tudesko."

Hocus-Pocus was a famous juggler of the times.

"Who's Travitanto Tudesko, boy?" Damplay asked.

John Trygust answered:

"Another juggler with a long name."

He then said:

"I wish either that those expecters you talk about would be gone hence now, at the first act, or that they would expect no more hereafter than they understand."

"Why so, my peremptory jack?" Damplay said.

He felt that the theater boy was peremptory: overly confident in his opinions.

The theater boy — John Trygust — said:

"My name is John, indeed."

The name "Jack" is a nickname for "John."

John Trygust continued:

"My answer to your question is this: Because those who expect what is impossible or beyond nature defraud and cheat themselves."

"There the boy said well: They do defraud and cheat themselves indeed," Probee said.

John Trygust said:

"And therefore, Master Damplay, unless, like a solemn justice of wit — a judge without a sense of humor — you will damn our play unheard or unexamined, I shall entreat your Mistress, Madam Expectation, if she is among these ladies, to have patience but a pissing while — a short time, the time it takes to piss — in order to give our springs leave to open a little by degrees!

"A source of ridiculous, laughter-causing matter may break forth soon that shall steep their temples and bathe their brains in laughter, to the fomenting of stupidity itself and the awaking any velvet lethargy — well-dressed sleepy person — in the house."

Probee said, "Why do you maintain your poet's quarrel so with velvet and good clothes, boy? We have seen him in indifferent — neither especially good nor especially bad — clothes before now."

The poet was Ben Jonson.

John Trygust said:

"And you may see him in better clothing, if it please the King, his master, to say amen and agree to it, and allow it, to whom he acknowledges all."

If the King were to — ahem — give Ben Jonson more money, Ben Jonson would dress better.

John Trygust continued:

"But his clothes shall never be the best thing about him, though; he will have something in addition, either of humane letters and classical learning or severe honesty, that shall speak and reveal him to be a man even if he went about naked."

For some people, their clothes — not their mind — are the best thing about them. This is not the case with Ben Jonson.

"He is beholden to you, if you can make this good, boy," Probee said. "If you can do it, the author will owe much to you, boy."

"He himself has done that already against envy," John Trygust said.

Ben Jonson had criticized malicious envy in the induction of his play *The Arraignment, or Poetaster*.

In his plays, poems, and masques, Ben Jonson had shown that he was worthy of great respect no matter what clothes — if any — he was wearing.

"What's your name, sir, or your country?" Damplay asked.

"John Trygust is my name," the theater-boy said. "I am a Cornish youth, and I am the poet's servant."

The poet, of course, is Ben Jonson.

"West-country breed, I thought, you were so bold," Damplay said.

John Trygust said, "Or rather saucy, to find out your palate, Master Damplay. Indeed, we do call a spade a spade in Cornwall. If you dare damn our play in the wrong place, we shall take heart — have the courage — to tell you so."

"Good boy!" Probee said.

CHAPTER 2
— 2.1 —

Nurse Keep, Placentia, and Pleasance spoke together in a room in Lady Loadstone's house.

Nurse Keep said to Placentia, "Sweet mistress, please be merry. You are sure to have a husband now."

"Aye, if the store does not hurt the choice," Placentia replied.

Placentia had a store — an abundance — of suitors: Sir Diaphanous Silkworm the courtier and Master Practice the lawyer. And now, although she did not know it yet, Master Bias.

A plenitude of suitors could make deciding among them difficult.

"Store is no sore, young mistress, my mother is wont to say," Pleasance said.

By "my mother," she meant "Mistress Polish."

The proverb "Store is no sore" means "Abundance is not a problem."

"And she'll say as wisely as any mouth in the parish," Nurse Keep said. "Fix on one, fix upon one, good mistress. Choose a suitor to marry."

"At this call, too, here's Master Practice who is called to the bench of purpose," Placentia said.

Master Practice was called to Lady Loadstone's dinner-table for the purpose of being a suitor.

Nurse Keep said, "Yes, and by My Lady's means —"

Lady Loadstone had encouraged Master Practice to court Placentia and to come to the dinner.

"He is thought to be the man who will marry you," Pleasance said to Placentia.

One purpose of Lady Loadstone's dinner was to decide on a husband for Placentia. Placentia's preference among the suitors counted for something, but if she rejected Lady Loadstone's suitors for her, she could lose her marriage portion. The decisive vote was that of her mother: Lady Loadstone.

Nurse Keep said, "A lawyer's wife —"

Pleasance added, "— and a fine lawyer's wife —"

Nurse Keep concluded, "— is a brave and fine calling."

"Calling" is a form of address: what one is called. Often, one's calling includes a title.

"Sweet Mistress Practice!" Pleasance said.

"Gentle Mistress Practice!" Nurse Keep said.

"Fair, open Mistress Practice!" Pleasance said.

"Open" means "free and frank," among other meanings.

"Aye, and close and cunning Mistress Practice!" Nurse Keep said.

"Close" means "secretive."

"Cunning" means "wise and crafty."

"I don't like that 'Mistress Practice,'" Placentia said. "The courtier's is the neater — more elegant — calling."

Yes, she would be called "Lady" if she married the courtier.

"Yes, My Lady Silkworm," Pleasance said.

"And to shine in plush," Nurse Keep said.

"Plush" is an expensive fabric.

"Like a young night-crow, a Diaphanous Silkworm," Pleasance said.

"Night-crows" are nocturnal birds of ill omen.

Courtiers such as Diaphanous Silkworm keep late hours and sleep late.

"The title 'Lady Diaphanous' sounds most delicate and delightful!" Nurse Keep said.

Actually, she would be Lady Placentia Silkworm.

"Which suitor would you choose now, mistress?" Pleasance asked.

"I cannot say," Placentia said. "The copious abundance of suitors does confound and confuse one."

"Here's my mother," Pleasance said.

Mistress Polish entered the scene.

She said, "How are things now, my dainty charge of delicate health and my diligent nurse? What were you chanting — chattering — about?"

A "charge" is a responsibility.

Pleasance, her daughter, knelt before her to receive her blessing.

"God bless you, maiden," Mistress Polish said to her.

Pleasance rose.

Nurse Keep said, "All of us were enchanting, wishing for a husband for my young mistress here. A man to please her."

"She shall have a man, good nurse, and she must have a man: a man and a half, if we can choose him out," Mistress Polish said.

"A man and a half" is better than just a man.

"A man and a half" also means a man and a better half.

She continued:

"We are all in council within and sit about it: the doctors and the scholars and My Lady, who's wiser than all of us.

"Where's Master Needle? Her Ladyship needs him to prick out the man."

Master Needle was Lady Loadstone's steward and tailor.

Needles can be used to prick, but Master Needle was needed now to prick — choose — the name of the man who would marry Placentia. They were sitting in council to make that choice, and when the choice was made, Master Needle could metaphorically prick — mark — the man's name. Think of a list of names written on a wax tablet.

Pleasance exited to get Master Needle.

Mistress Polish said to Placentia:

"How is my sweet young mistress?

"You don't look well, I think. How are you, dear charge?

"You must have a husband, and you shall have a husband. There's two men put forward as choices for making a match with you. And there's a third man your uncle promises."

That third suitor, put forward by Sir Moth Interest, was Master Bias.

Mistress Polish continued:

"But you must still be ruled by your aunt, according to the will of your dead father and mother, who are in heaven.

"Your lady aunt has choice in the house — within the family — for you.

"We do not trust your uncle. He would keep you a bachelor — an unmarried maiden — always so he can keep control of your marriage portion — your dowry — and keep you not only without a husband, but with a sickness.

"Aye, and I mean the green sickness, the maiden's malady, which is a sickness, a kind of a disease, I can assure you, and like the fish our mariners call remora —"

A remora was a fish that was believed to attach itself to a ship and slow its progress.

According to the *Oxford English Dictionary*, a remora is "Any of various slender marine fishes of the family Echeneidae, which have the dorsal fin modified to form a large oval suction disc for attachment to the undersides of sharks, other large fishes, cetaceans, and turtles."

Never being married can retard a woman's progress when she lives in a society where she is expected to marry and have children.

Nurse Keep interrupted, "— a remora, mistress!"

Annoyed, Mistress Polish, said:

"How now, goody nurse, Dame Keep of Kat'er'ne's?"

"Goody" is short for "goodwife," a title of address.

She was referring to Saint Katherine's Hospital, where insane people were kept.

"Kat'er'ne's" may also be an oblique reference to "cater'in's," or "caterwaulings."

Nurse Keep was doing a fair amount of caterwauling

Mistress Polish continued:

"What! Have you an oar in the cockboat because you are a sailor's wife and come from Shadwell? I say a remora, for it will stay and delay a ship that's under sail."

A cockboat is a small boat.

"Shadwell" is a dock that had a bad reputation.

"An oar in the cockboat" may have a bawdy meaning.

Master Needle entered the scene, accompanied by Pleasance.

Mistress Polish continued:

"And stays and delays are long and tedious things to maidens! And maidens are young ships that would be sailing when they are rigged. For what reason is all their trim else?"

"Stays" and "rigging" are ship ropes.

"Stays" are also 1) delays, and 2) a corset's stiffening support.

Removing a corset can delay a maiden who is eager to cease being a maiden (a virgin).

A rig is a wanton woman. A rigged woman is a well-dressed woman.

"Trim" can refer to 1) a ship's being trimmed: rigged and ready to sail, or 2) good clothing.

Master Needle said, "True, and for them to be stayed —"

"The stay is dangerous," Mistress Polish said. "You know it, Master Needle."

Master Needle said, "I know something, I can assure you, from the doctor's mouth.

"Placentia has a dropsy, and she must have a change of air before she can recover."

Mistress Polish asked him, "Do you say so, sir?"

"The doctor says so," Master Needle said.

Mistress Polish said:

"Says His Worship so?

"I warrant them he says the truth then; doctors are sometimes soothsayers and are always cunning-men.

"Which doctor was it?"

"Even My Lady's doctor," Master Needle said, "the neat — skillful — house-doctor. But he is a true stone-doctor."

Stone-horses still had their testicles; they were not geldings.

Mistress Polish said:

"Why, do you hear this, nurse? How comes this gear — this trouble — to happen?

"This is your fault, in truth. It shall be your fault, and it must be your fault.

"Why is your mistress sick?

"She had her health all the time she was with me."

Nurse Keep said, "Alas, good Mistress Polish, I am no saint, much less am I My Lady, to be urged to give health or sickness at my will, but I must await the stars' good pleasure and I must do my duty."

In other words: She lacked the power of the Fates and of Lady Loadstone and instead had to do her duty and hope for illness to be warded off, and when illness occurred, she had to hope for healing to occur.

Mistress Polish said, "You must do more than your duty, foolish nurse! You must do all you can — and more than you can, more than is possible — when folks are sick, especially when the sick person is a mistress, a young mistress."

Doctor Rut and Lady Loadstone entered the room.

Nurse Keep said, "Here's Master Doctor himself, who cannot do that."

She exited.

Madame Polish said, "Doctor Do-all can do it. That's why he's called that."

Mistress Polish had faith in Doctor Rut: He could do anything.

"Do," however, can mean "have sex with." The word "rut" also refers to sex.

Doctor Rut asked about "Doctor Do-All," "Where is he from? What's he called?"

Mistress Polish said, "Doctor, do all you can, I pray you and beseech you, for my charge here."

Lady Loadstone said about Mistress Polish, "She's my tendering gossip, my affectionate friend, and she loves and attends to my niece."

"I know you can do all things, what you please, sir, for a young damsel, My good Lady's niece here," Mistress Polish said. "You can do what you wish."

"Peace, tiffany," Doctor Rut said.

Tiffany is a flimsy fabric: Doctor Rut was insulting Mistress Polish.

"Especially in this new case of the dropsy," Mistress Polish said. "The gentlewoman, I fear, is leavened."

Leavened bread has yeast: It rises. Think of a loaf of bread in the oven.

"Leavened?" Doctor Rut asked. "What's that?"

Mistress Polish answered, "Puffed, blown, if it please Your Worship."

"What!" Doctor Rut said. "Dark by darker? What is blown? Puffed? Speak English —"

Mistress Polish's explanation of her comment was harder to understand than her original comment.

In English: Placentia's belly was swollen.

Mistress Polish continued not speaking English:

"Tainted, if it please you, some do call it."

In other words: Placentia's belly was contaminated, corrupted.

Mistress Polish finally spoke English:

"She swells and swells so with it —"

Doctor Rut said

"Give her vent — an outlet — if she do swell. A gimlet that will make a hole must be had.

"It is tympanites that she is troubled with.

"There are three kinds.

"The first kind is anasarca [dropsy of the abdomen] under the flesh, a tumor: That's not her kind.

"The second is ascites, or *aquosus*, a watery humor: That's not her kind either.

"But her kind is a tympanites, which we call the drum.

"A wind bomb's in her belly; it must be unbraced and loosened, and with a faucet — a tap — or a peg let the wind bomb out, and she'll do well. Get her a husband."

The faucet and peg are phallic symbols. They will drill a hole in Placentia and let the "wind bomb" out.

Mistress Polish said, "Yes, I say so, Master Doctor, and betimes — quickly — too."

Yes, get Placentia a husband quickly.

"As soon as we can," Lady Loadstone said. "Let her bear up and keep up her spirits today, laugh, and keep company at gleek or crimp."

Gleek and crimp are card games. The names of the games refer to tricks and traps.

"Your Ladyship says the right thing," Mistress Polish said. "Crimp, surely, will cure her."

Doctor Rut said:

"Yes, and gleek, too.

"Peace and silence, Gossip Tittle-Tattle — Gossip Chatterbox.

"Placentia must tomorrow go down into the country some twenty miles. She must use a coach and six brave — splendid — horses, take the fresh air a month there, or five weeks, and then return as a new bride up to the town for any husband in the hemisphere to chuck at, when she has dropped her tympany."

The husband could chuckle at her or gently chuck — tap — her under the chin.

The hemisphere is the part of the heavens that can be seen above the horizon.

"Drop" can mean 1) "get rid of," or 2) "let fall."

"Must she then drop it?" Mistress Polish asked.

Doctor Rut said:

"That is why it is called a dropsy.

"The tympanites is one spice of — a touch of — it: It is a toy, a trifle, a thing of nothing, a mere vapor.

"I'll blow it away."

Lady Loadstone said, "Needle, you get the coach ready for tomorrow morning."

"Yes, madam," Master Needle said.

Master Needle and Pleasance exited.

"I'll go down with her into the country myself and thank the doctor," Lady Loadstone said.

"We all shall thank him," Mistress Polish said. "But, dear madam, think and resolve upon a man this day. Decide who the bridegroom will be."

Lady Loadstone said:

"I have done it.

"To tell you true, sweet gossip — nobody is here except Master Doctor; he shall be of the council — the man I have designated for her, indeed, is Master Practice. He's a neat — skillful — young man, forward and eager, ambitious, and precocious, and growing up in a profession in which he is likely to be somebody important, if Westminster Hall continues to stand and the pleading of law cases continues.

"To be a prime young lawyer's wife is a very happy fortune."

Doctor Rut said:

"And since she is bringing so plentiful a marriage portion, they may live like a king and a queen at common law together."

He meant that they would have an interest in law together as a source of livelihood, but the phrase also has the meaning that they could have a marriage that is recognized by common law.

Doctor Rut continued:

"They may sway judges; guide the courts; command the clerks and frighten the evidence; and rule at their pleasures, like petty sovereigns in all cases!"

"Sway judges?" "Guide the courts?" Hmm. Placentia's dowry would give them enough money to sway and guide — that is, bribe — judges, jurors, and clerks.

"Frighten the evidence"? Hmm. Sounds like they would intimidate the witnesses.

Mistress Polish said:

"Oh, that will be a work of time. It will take a long while to achieve that! She may be old before her husband rises to the position of being a chief judge, and all her metaphorical flower will be gone.

"No, no, I would have her be a lady of the first head and in the royal court."

A deer with its first set of antlers is said to have its first head. Metaphorically, new nobles would be of the first head.

Mistress Polish continued:

"I would have her be the Lady Silkworm, a diaphanous lady, and she would be a viscountess to carry all before her, as we say.

"Her gentleman-usher and cast-off pages will be bare to bid her aunt welcome to Her Honor at her lodgings."

Given her dropsy, Placentia would be carrying her big belly in front of her and in front of everyone.

The gentleman-usher and pages would be bare-headed.

"Cast-off pages" are freely-moving pages; they are like dogs that have slipped — cast off — their leashes.

Readers with a bawdy mind may think that Placentia is a vice-cunt-woman — viscountess — and that the gentleman-usher and pages are bare-naked. They may also think that the pages are cast-off — former — lovers.

Yes, playwrights of the early 1600s were that bawdy.

Doctor Rut said, "You say well, lady's gossip, if My Lady could admit and accept that and be willing to have her niece precede her."

A viscountess would rank high socially — higher than Lady Loadstone.

Lady Loadstone was the widow of a knight, and so she was a gentlewoman, but a viscountess was the wife of a viscount, and so she was a noblewoman.

"For that, I must consult my own ambition, my zealous gossip," Lady Loadstone said.

Mistress Polish said:

"Oh, you shall precede her: You shall be a countess.

"Sir Diaphanous shall get you made a countess. He will find a count for you to marry."

Seeing Sir Diaphanous Silkworm coming, she said:

"Here he comes, he has my voice — vote — certainly — O fine courtier! O blessèd man! The bravery pricked out — the splendid man chosen — to make my dainty charge a viscountess!"

A different kind of "prick" out would make Placentia a viscountess: A consummated marriage to Sir Diaphanous Silkworm would make her a viscountess.

Mistress Polish continued:

"And to make My good Lady, her aunt, countess at large!"

Readers with a bawdy mind can think that "countess at large" means sexually available cunt-ess.

The non-bawdy meaning is that Lady Loadstone will be widely recognized in society.

Sir Diaphanous Silkworm and Parson Palate entered the scene and spoke together apart from the others. Placentia had a dowry of sixteen thousand pounds, and Sir Diaphanous was willing to bribe other people so he could get it.

Sir Diaphanous Silkworm said, "I tell thee, parson, if I get her, you can reckon thou have a friend in court and shall command a thousand pounds to go on any errand — any quest — for any church preferment thou have a mind to."

A proverb stated, "Better is a friend in court than a penny in purse."

Sir Diaphanous Silkworm was bribing Parson Palate with money: a thousand pounds that he could use for expenses in seeking promotions.

Those expenses could include bribery. The use of bribes to secure advancement in ecclesiastical circles is called simony. If simony were to be discovered in the election of a pope, that election would be null and void.

Parson Palate said:

"I thank Your Worship. I will so work for you that you shall study and investigate all the ways to thank me. I'll work on and persuade My Lady and My Lady's friends: her gossip, and this doctor, and Squire Needle, and Master Compass, who is all in all — he is all-important to her, and the very fly she moves by."

A fly is a component of a sailor's compass. A compass points out the way for one to go.

Parson Palate continued:

"He is one who went to sea with her husband, Sir John Loadstone, and brought home the rich prizes."

Prizes are ships captured during a war.

Parson Palate continued:

"All that wealth has been left to her, for which service she respects him, a dainty — excellent — scholar in the mathematics and one she wholly employs — relies on — to advise her.

"Now Dominus [Lord] Practice is already the man appointed by Her Ladyship, but there's a trick to set his cap awry and interfere with him and his expectations, if I know anything.

"He has confessed to me in private that he loves another, My Lady's serving-woman, Mistress Pleasance; therefore, that makes you safe from his rivalship. You won't have to worry about him being your rival."

"I thank thee, my noble parson," Sir Diaphanous Silkworm said. "There's five hundred pounds more that waits on thee for that. You'll receive that much more money."

Parson Palate said:

"Accost the niece. Yonder she walks alone."

"Accost" means "board her" as if she were a prize to be captured — "woo her."

Parson Palate continued:

"I'll move — persuade — the aunt.

"But here's the gossip, her friend: She expects a morsel.

"Haven't you a ring or a toy — a trifle — to throw away?"

"Yes, here's a diamond of some threescore pounds," Sir Diaphanous Silkworm said. "Please give her that."

He handed the parson a diamond.

"If she will take it," Parson Palate said.

Sir Diaphanous Silkworm said:

"And there's an emerald for the doctor, too."

He handed over the emerald and then said:

"Thou, parson, thou shall coin me: I am thine. You shall make money out of me."

Parson Palate said:

"Here Master Compass comes."

Compass entered the scene.

Parson Palate said about him:

"Do you see My Lady and all the rest? How they do flutter about him! He is the oracle — the prophet and seer — of the house and family.

"Now is your time: Go nick it with the niece — take advantage of this opportunity."

A nick is a winning throw in the dice game called Hazard.

Parson Palate then said:

"I will walk by and hearken how the chimes go. I will hear how things are going."

Sir Diaphanous Silkworm began to court Placentia at the side of the room.

Seeing Parson Palate, Compass said:

"Nay, parson, don't stand far off; you may approach.

"This is no such hidden point of state we handle, but you may hear it, for we are all of counsel."

In other words: Come join us. We are not discussing a matter of national importance that we must keep secret from you.

"We are all of counsel" means "We are all in the know."

Parson Palate walked over to the group.

Compass then said to Lady Loadstone, "The gentle Master Practice has dealt clearly and nobly with you, madam."

"Have you talked with him, and made the overture?" Lady Loadstone asked.

The overture concerned marriage to Placentia. It was the opening gambit in a negotiation.

Compass said:

"Yes, first I put forward the business entrusted to me by Your Ladyship in your own words, almost your very syllables, except where my memory trespassed against their elegance and I forgot the elegant words you used and was forced to use my own words, for which I hope to have your pardon.

"Then I enlarged and spoke more fully about the advantages of marriage with Placentia in my own plain and homely style: the special goodness and greatness of your bounty in your choice and the free and voluntary conferring of a benefit so without concealed ends and ulterior purposes and conditions, and without any tie except his pure virtue.

"And I spoke about the value and worth of this marriage, to call him into your kindred, into your veins and bloodline, insert him into your immediate family, and make him a nephew by the offer of a niece with such a marriage portion.

"When he had heard this and most maturely acknowledged (as his professional training in the profession of law tends to make every matter a matter of due and mature deliberation), he returned a thanks as ample as the courtesy, in my opinion.

"He said it was a grace too great to be rejected or accepted by him.

"But as the terms stood and made common cause with his fortune, he was not to prevaricate and be evasive with Your Ladyship, but rather to require ingenious — noble, honest, and frank — permission that he might, with the same love and goodwill with which it was offered, refuse it, since he could not with his honesty — because he was engaged before — receive it."

Master Practice had rejected the offer of marriage to Placentia.

This kind of engagement is attraction to another woman whom he would like to marry: His love was engaged.

"The same he said to me," Parson Palate said.

"And did he name the party?" Compass asked.

The "party" is the woman Master Practice wanted instead of Placentia.

"He did, and he did not," Parson Palate said.

Possibly, he did not name the woman he loved. Also possibly, however, the name of the woman he loved could be guessed.

"Come, leave your schemes and fine amphibolies, parson," Compass said.

"Fine amphibolies" are deliberate ambiguities.

"You'll hear more," Parson Palate said.

"Why, now Your Ladyship is free to choose the courtier, Sir Diaphanous: He shall do it. I'll put it forward to him myself," Mistress Polish said.

"What will you put forward to him?" Lady Loadstone asked.

"The making you a countess," Mistress Polish said.

"Stint and stop, foolish woman," Lady Loadstone said.

Mistress Polish went to the side to join Placentia and Sir Diaphanous Silkworm.

Lady Loadstone asked Compass, "Do you know the party Master Practice means?"

Compass replied, "No, but your parson says he knows, madam."

Lady Loadstone replied, "I fear he fables — I fear he invents things."

She then asked, "Parson, do you know where Master Practice is engaged?"

Parson Palate said:

"I'll tell you, but under seal — in strict confidence. Her mother must not know.

"It is with Your Ladyship's serving-woman, Mistress Pleasance."

"What!" Compass said.

"He is not mad?" Lady Loadstone said.

Master Practice could be mad because he has chosen a woman who has no dowry, or he could be not mad because he has chosen to love a good woman.

Or it is Compass who could be mad for a not-yet-revealed reason.

"Oh, hide the hideous secret from her mother: Mistress Polish!" Parson Palate said. "She'll trouble all, otherwise. You hold a cricket by the wing."

Proverbially, to hold a cricket or a grasshopper by the wing means to endure much noise.

"Did he name Pleasance?" Compass said. "Are you sure, parson?"

Lady Loadstone said:

"Oh, it is true! He named your mistress: the woman to whom you are devoted!

"I find where your shoe wrings you, Master Compass. I have found your sensitive spot.

"But you'll look to him there and put him right. You will take care of your rival."

Compass was also interested in Pleasance.

Master Practice entered the scene in the company of Sir Moth Interest and Master Bias. They were talking together.

Compass said, "Yes. Here's Sir Moth, your brother, with his Bias and the party deep in discourse. It will be about making a bargain and sale, I see by their close working of their heads and running them together so in counsel."

He knew that they were bargaining about Placentia and whom she would marry. They had put their heads together and were quietly negotiating.

"Will Master Practice be of counsel against us?" Lady Loadstone asked. "Will he be hired in his professional position to be against us?"

Sir Moth Interest could hire him in an attempt to keep Placentia's marriage portion — or most of it.

Compass said:

"He is a lawyer, and he must speak for his fee against his father and mother, all his kindred, his brothers or his sisters.

"No exception — or objection — lies at the common law."

In other words: As a lawyer, Master Practice must speak as he has been paid to speak: whether for or against. He had to speak for the side that had retained him. Natural affections such as familial ties must have no effect on his profession.

Compass continued:

"He must not alter nature for form."

In other words: He has a nature (a capacity and talent) for form (legal procedures), and he must not alter it. That is, he must not allow such things as natural affections and familial ties to have an effect on how he performs in his profession.

Compass continued:

"Instead, he must go on in his path — it may be he will be for us and on our side.

"Don't attempt to meddle.

"Let them take their course; let them dispatch and marry her off to any husband.

"Don't be over-scrupulous. Don't be overly particular.

"Let who can, have her, as long as Sir Moth lays down the marriage portion, though he geld it."

Compass was advising that Placentia be married to any man who could get her dowry — or part of it — out of the hands of Sir Moth Interest.

Compass continued:

"It will maintain the lawsuit against him later if he holds back part of the dowry. To some extent, something in the hand is better than no birds."

A proverb stated, "A bird in the hand is worth two in the bush."

Compass hoped to get more than one metaphorical bird for Placentia: one "bird" now in the form of part of her dowry, and the other "bird or birds" in the form of the rest of her dowry after a successful lawsuit against Sir Moth Interest.

Compass continued:

"He shall at last — eventually — account for the utmost farthing, if you can keep your hand from signing any discharge or release of obligation."

Lady Loadstone exited.

Mistress Polish said to Sir Diaphanous Silkworm, "Sir, do but make her worshipful aunt a countess, and Placentia is yours. Her aunt has worlds to leave you! The wealth of six East Indian fleets of merchant ships at least! Her husband, Sir John Loadstone, was the governor of the East India Company for seven years."

"And came there home six fleets of ships in seven years?" Sir Diaphanous Silkworm asked.

"I cannot tell," Mistress Polish said. "I must attend my gossip, Her good Ladyship."

She exited.

Placentia asked:

"And will you make me a viscountess, too?

"For how do they make a countess? In a chair?"

Can a court official rule that a woman is a countess?

She then asked:

"Or upon a bed?"

Yes, marry a count and you will be made a countess in bed.

A chair can also be the location where a marriage to a count is consummated.

Sir Diaphanous Silkworm answered, "Both ways, sweet bird: I'll show you."

Placentia and Sir Diaphanous exited.

Sir Moth Interest said:

"The truth is, Master Practice, now that we are sure that you are off the list and not a suitor, we dare come on the bolder:

"The portion left was sixteen thousand pounds — I do confess it as a just man should — and I call here Master Compass with these gentlemen to the relation."

Compass and these other gentlemen were supposed to listen to the financial report, too.

Sir Moth Interest continued:

"I will continue to be just.

"Now as for the profits every way arising, it was the donor's wisdom that those profits should pay me for my watchful wakefulness and the breaking of my sleeps.

"It is no petty charge and responsibility, you know, that sum. It will keep a man wakeful for fourteen years."

Placentia was fourteen years old, and Sir Moth Interest had controlled her money for fourteen years.

Worrying about investments can result in poor sleep.

Master Practice said, "But, as you knew to use it in that time, it would reward your waking."

Master Practice was pointing out that as a skilled usurer, Sir Moth Interest would be well rewarded for using that money in usury.

Sir Moth Interest said:

"That's my industry and diligence, as it might be your reading, study, and counsel, and now your pleading — your argument.

"Who denies your calling to you?

"I have my calling, too.

"Well, sir, the contract is with this gentleman, ten thousand pounds — an ample portion for a younger brother, with a soft, tender, delicate rib of man's flesh that he may work like wax and print upon.

The "rib of man's flesh" is a wife, as Eve was to Adam.

The husband may work her like wax and shape her as he pleases and print upon her by making her pregnant.

These days, we may want to call a pregnant woman's uterus and vagina a biological 3-D printer.

Sir Moth Interest continued:

"He expects no more than that sum to be tendered if he shall receive it: Those are the conditions."

Sir Moth Interest wanted Master Practice to be the lawyer for Master Bias and him. Sir Moth Interest wanted Master Bias to marry Placentia and receive ten thousand pounds as her dowry. Sir Moth Interest would receive the remaining six thousand pounds of the dowry. Master Practice, of course, would be paid for his representation of and advocacy of the interests of Sir Moth Interest and Master Bias. And, readers will soon see, Sir Moth Interest wanted to receive much more than six thousand pounds.

"A direct bargain and in open sale in the market," Master Practice said.

Sir Moth Interest said, "And what I have furnished him with on the side to appear or so: a matter of four hundred pounds, to be deducted upon the payment —"

Sir Moth Interest had advanced 400 pounds to Master Bias so that he could make a good appearance.

Master Bias interrupted, "Right. You deal like a just man still."

"Write up this contract, good Master Practice, for us to sign, and be speedy," Sir Moth Interest said.

Master Practice said:

"But here's a mighty gain, sir, you have made of this one stock — this one dowry. The principal first doubled in the first seven years, and that redoubled in the next seven years!

"Besides six thousand pounds, there's threescore thousand got in fourteen years after the usual rate of ten in the hundred, and the ten thousand paid."

Through usury, Sir Moth Interest had made Placentia's marriage portion grow.

At ten percent interest, 16,000 pounds had become 32,000 pounds in seven years, and 32,000 pounds had become 64,000 pounds in the next seven years.

Sir Moth Interest wanted Master Bias to get 10,000 pounds. The remaining 54,000 pounds (which includes the 6,000 pounds already discussed) would be Sir Moth Interest's.

Of course, Sir Moth Interest was to be paid for his watchfulness in investing the money, but why wouldn't much of the increase in the amount of money go to Placentia and her husband?

"I think it is so," Sir Moth Interest said.

"How will you escape the clamor and the envy?" Master Practice said.

There would an outcry (clamor) and ill will (envy) against Sir Moth Interest getting so much. It would be a major scandal.

Lady Loadstone, Compass, and others had been afraid that Sir Moth Interest would attempt to do something like this. They wanted the money to go to Placentia and her husband.

Sir Moth Interest said:

"Let them exclaim and envy. What do I care?

"Their murmurs and complaints raise no blisters in my flesh."

In other words: Their words cannot raise welts on his flesh.

Sir Moth Interest continued:

"My moneys are my blood, my parents, and my kindred, and whoever does not love those is unnatural.

"I am persuaded that the love of money is not a virtue only in a subject, but also that it might befit a prince.

"And, if need be, I find that I would be able to make good the assertion to any reasonable man's understanding and make him believe and confess it."

Sir Moth Interest was going against scripture.

1 Timothy 6:10 states, *"For the love of money is the root of all evil: which while some coveted after, they have erred from the faith, and pierced themselves through with many sorrows"* (King James Version).

Compass said, "Gentlemen, doctors, and scholars, you'll hear this and see as much true secular and worldly wit and deep lay sense as can be shown on such a commonplace."

A commonplace is a topic for a debate or a sermon. It is a general truth or "truth" that the speaker defends.

Sir Moth Interest began his argument that love of money is a virtue:

"First, we all know the soul of man is infinite in what it covets. A man who desires knowledge desires it infinitely. A man who covets honor covets it infinitely.

"It will be then no hard thing for a coveting man to prove or to confess he aims at infinite wealth."

Point One: Human beings want the infinite: some in knowledge, some in honor, some in wealth.

"His soul lying that way," Compass said.

The word "lying" can mean 1) inclining toward, or 2) telling lies.

Sir Moth Interest continued his argument:

"Next, and secondly, every man is in the hope or possibility of a whole, complete, perfect world, this present world being nothing but the dispersèd issue — result — of the first one."

The first world is the Garden of Eden before the fall.

Sir Moth Interest continued his argument:

"And therefore I do not see but a just man may with just reason and out of duty propound to himself —"

Point Two: Every man hopes to become wealthy just as they hope to return to a world such as the Garden of Eden. The Garden of Eden is perfect, and infinite wealth is part of a perfect world.

"An infinite wealth!" Compass said. "I'll bear the burden."

Compass would the bear the burden of being wealthy, and he would bear the burden — sing the chorus — to Sir Moth Interest's verses.

Compass then said: "Go on, Sir Moth."

Sir Moth Interest continued his argument:

"Thirdly, if we consider man a member but of the body politic — a citizen — we know, by just experience, that the prince has need more of one wealthy man than ten fighting men."

"There you went out of the road a little from us," Compass said.

Compass was not wealthy, but he was in part a soldier.

Sir Moth Interest continued his argument:

"And therefore, if the prince's aims be infinite, it must be in that which makes all —"

Compass interrupted, "— infinite wealth."

Point Three: Money facilitates everything, and so a ruler needs wealthy men to tax. The ruler needs them much more than he needs soldiers to fight.

Sir Moth Interest continued his argument:

"Fourthly, it is natural to all good subjects to set a price on money —"

The word "natural" can mean 1) appropriate, or 2) foolish.

People really do put a value on money. In fact, the value of a coin is literally put on coins.

Sir Moth Interest continued his argument:

"— more than fools ought on their mistress' picture, every piece from the penny to the twelvepence being the hieroglyphic and sacred sculpture — the sacred symbol and the engraving — of the sovereign."

Point Four: The image of the sovereign is stamped on coins. Citizens love their sovereign, and so they love coins.

"A manifest and clearly revealed conclusion, and a safe one," Compass said.

It is not safe to run afoul of royalty, and so it is best to praise royalty.

Sir Moth Interest continued his argument:

"Fifthly, wealth gives a man the leading voice at all conventions and public meetings, and it displaces worth and merit with general allowance to all parties."

In other words: Wealth is generally believed to outweigh virtue. It can also outweigh social rank. Wealthy people are respected, and they are listened to.

Sir Moth Interest continued his argument:

"Wealth makes a trade — a business — take the wall of virtue."

"To take the wall" means "to take the best position." Higher-ranking people took the position closest to the wall. Those walking further from the wall were in danger of being splashed with muddy water from the street. A wealthy businessman could take the wall.

Since trade and business take the wall instead of virtue, wealth gotten from trade and business is valued more highly than virtue.

Sir Moth Interest continued his fifth argument:

"Wealth makes the mere issue of a shop right honorable."

The wealthy child of a shopkeeper can become a right honorable lord.

Point Five: Wealth gives shopkeepers and merchants influence. People who have money can speak freely. They are also respected and their children can rise high in social rank.

Sir Moth Interest continued his argument:

"Sixthly, it enables him who has it to do the performance of all real actions, referring him to himself always, and not binding his will to any circumstance without considering himself and his interests."

In other words: Wealth enables a person to perform every action in such a way that it benefits himself; he need not perform actions that don't benefit himself. A wealthy man need not sell his time and labor to someone else unless he wants to and will benefit from doing so.

Sir Moth Interest continued his argument:

"It gives him precise knowledge of himself, for, if he is rich, he straightaway with evidence knows whether he has any compassion or any inclination to virtue or not."

Point Six: Wealth allows people to know themselves. If a wealthy man is virtuous, he will do virtuous things with his wealth. If he is not virtuous, he will not do virtuous things with his wealth. What he chooses to do with his money will tell him much about himself.

Sir Moth Interest continued his sixth argument:

"Whereas the poor knave — the ordinary man — erroneously believes, if he were rich, he would build churches or do such mad things."

According to Sir Moth Interest, it is mad to do such things as build churches.

Point Six, Part 2: Poor people always delude themselves into thinking that if they were wealthy, they would be virtuous.

Sir Moth Interest continued his argument:

"Seventhly, your wise poor men have always been contented to observe rich fools and so to serve their turns upon them, subjecting all their wit to the others' wealth and become gentlemen parasites, squire bawds, to feed their patrons' honorable humors."

Point Seven: Wise but poor men will work for the wealthy but foolish man. They will use their intelligence to serve the wealthy but foolish man in return for sustenance.

Sir Moth Interest continued his argument:

"Eighthly, it is certain that a man may leave his wealth either to his children or his friends.

"His wit and intelligence he cannot so dispose by legacy as they shall be a harington — a brass farthing — the better for it."

Point Eight: A man who has read and understood 10,000 books cannot pass on that knowledge to his children when he dies. They will have to read books on their own. Wealth, in contrast, can be passed on to children.

"A man of wit and intelligence may entail a jest upon his house, though —" Compass said.

Captain Ironside entered the scene. Among those present were Sir Moth Interest, Parson Palate, Doctor Rut, and Master Bias.

Compass continued, "—or leave a tale to his posterity to be told after him."

Compass' words are true:

- Harry Lehr, aka America's Court Jester, got married, but he later grew to hate his wife. When he died, his will stated that he had left her "my houses, lands, silver plate, tapestries, pictures, carriages, yachts and motor cars." However, Mr. Lehr didn't own any of that stuff.

- John Custis hated being married to his wife, Fidelia. When he died, his tombstone stated that although he was 71 years old, he had lived only seven years — the years he had been an adult bachelor.

Ironside said:

"As you have done here?

"To invite your friend and brother to a feast where all the guests are so mere heterogene — so completely different — and such strangers that no man knows another man, or cares if those who here are met are Christians or Mohammedans!"

Compass asked, "Is it anything to you, brother, to know religions more than those you fight for?"

Is it really necessary to know another man's religion?

Captain Ironside replied:

"Yes, and I need to know with whom I eat.

"I may get into a discussion, and how shall I have an argument with such men whom I know neither their humors nor their heresies, and I don't know which heresies are religions now and so received?"

Some heresies become accepted and so they become religions.

Captain Ironside continued:

"Here's no man among these who keeps a servant whom I can ask questions about his master, yet in the house, I hear it buzzed and rumored that there are a brace of — a pair of — doctors, a fool and a physician [Parson Palate and Doctor Rut], with a courtier who feeds on mulberry leaves like a true silkworm [Sir Diaphanous Silkworm], a lawyer [Master Practice], and a mighty money-bawd, Sir Moth, who has brought his politic Bias with him."

One species of mulberry is food for silkworms.

Captain Ironside continued:

"Bias is a man of a most animadverting — critical and censorious — humor, who, to endear himself to his lord, will tell him that you and I, or any of us who here are met, are all pernicious and destructive spirits and men of pestilent purpose meanly affected — disposed — toward the nation we live in; and he will beget himself a thanks with the great men of the time by breeding jealousies — suspicions — in them against us.

"Bias shall cross and thwart our fortunes, frustrate our endeavors, twice seven years after."

"These seven years day" is an idiom for a long time. "Twice seven years" is a very long time.

Bias' tricks will harm those whom he targets for a very long time.

"And this trick is called the cutting of throats with a whispering or a penknife."

The "trick" was figurative murder caused by spreading rumors orally or in writing. Penknives are small knives that were used to make quill pens to dip into ink and write with.

Captain Ironside drew his sword and said:

"I must cut Bias' throat now. I'm bound in honor and by the law of arms to see it done.

"I dare to do it, and I dare to profess openly the doing of it, being a deed to be done against such a rascal and rogue, who is the common offence — disgrace — grown of mankind and worthy to be torn up from society."

Captain Ironside wanted to kill Master Bias, whom he regarded as the common disgrace of all mankind. The world would be better if Bias were dead.

"You shall not do it here, sir," Compass said.

Captain Ironside asked:

"Why? Will you entreat yourself into a beating for him, my courteous brother?"

In other words: Do you intend to negotiate that I beat you instead of killing him?

Captain Ironside continued:

"If you will, get ready to fight.

"No man deserves it better, now I think about it, than you, who will keep consort — company — with such fiddlers [triflers], pragmatic [busy and interfering] flies, fools, publicans [tax gatherers], and moths [people drawn to temptations that can destroy them like a moth is drawn to a flame], and leave your honest and adopted brother!"

"Consort with such fiddlers" sounds like "concert with such fiddlers."

Sir Moth Interest said, "It would be best to call for help and raise the house against him to secure us and make us safe — he'll kill us all!"

"I love no blades in belts!" Parson Palate said.

Swords and daggers were placed in scabbards that hung from belts.

"Nor I!" Doctor Rut said.

Master Bias said, "I wish that I were again at my shop — my place of business — in court, safely stowed up with my politic bundles of papers!"

Sir Moth Interest, Parson Palate, Doctor Rut, and Master Bias exited in a panic.

"How they are scattered!" Compass said.

"They have run away like *cimici* into the crannies of a rotten bedstead," Captain Ironside said.

Cimici is Italian for bedbugs.

Cimici glances at vim-and-see: Show some vim and vigor and see them scatter.

Compass said, "I told you such a passage of events — including the sight of your sword — would disperse them, even if the house were their fee-simple in law — their absolute possession — and they were possessed of all the blessings in it."

Captain Ironside said, "Pray heaven they are not so frightened from their stomachs that My Lady's table will be disfurnished of the provisions!"

Captain Ironside still wanted to eat a meal.

Compass said:

"No, by this time the parson's calling all the covey again together.

A covey is literally a group of birds.

Seeing Pleasance coming, Compass said:

"Here comes good tidings!

Pleasance entered the scene and said, "Dinner's on the table."

Captain Ironside and Master Practice exited.

Compass and Pleasance remained behind, close together.

Compass proceeded to ask Pleasance if she were engaged to marry Master Practice, but he did so using legal terms that were taken out of their usual context. In doing so, he made a series of legal puns.

"Stay, Mistress Pleasance. I must ask you a question," Compass said. "Have you any suits in law?"

A suit in law can be a lawsuit, or it can be a suitor who is in the law profession.

"I, Master Compass?" Pleasance asked.

"Answer me briefly," Compass said. "It is dinner time."

"Briefly" can refer to a period of time or a limited number of words; it puns on "law brief."

Compass said, "They say you have retained brisk Master Practice here of your counsel."

Lawyers get retainers — preliminary payment of fees — to secure their services. A woman engaged to be married may give her fiancé a gift.

Compass continued:

"And they say you are to be joined a patentee with him."

"Joined with" can mean "entered into a contract with." That contract can be a marriage contract.

A "patentee" is someone who has been officially granted something.

"Joined with in what?" Pleasance asked. "Who says so? You are disposed to jest."

Compass said:

"No, I am in earnest."

"In earnest" can mean "with serious intent," but "earnest" can also mean money paid in order to secure a contract.

Compass continued:

"It is given out in the house that what I said is so, I assure you, but keep your right to yourself and do not acquaint a common lawyer with your case."

In this society, the word "quaint" can mean "cunt."

The word "case" can mean 1) law case, or 2) vagina.

Compass continued:

"If he once find the gap, a thousand will leap after."

"Gap" can mean "hole," and therefore "vagina."

The word "leap" can mean "have sex." In this society, brothels were called leaping-houses.

Compass concluded:

"I'll tell you more soon."

He exited.

Alone, Pleasance said, "This riddle shows a little like a love-trick, of one face, if I could understand it. I will study it."

Pleasance recognized that Compass was anxious about her virginity. This could be a love-trick: a way of showing that he was interested in her, or a way of tricking her into loving him.

Maybe the one face was a deceptive face.

Like many women, she sometimes had trouble understanding a man: Was he serious or not? Did he love her or not?

She exited.

— CHORUS 2 —

Damplay asked, "But whom does your poet mean now by this Master Bias? What lord's secretary does he purpose to impersonate and represent or to perstringe — censure and criticize?"

John Trygust replied, "You might as well ask me what alderman or alderman's mate — companion — he meant by Sir Moth Interest; or what eminent lawyer he meant by the ridiculous Master Practice, whose name he invented for laughter — invented as a joke — rather than for any offence or injury it can stick on the reverend professors of the law. And so the wise ones will think."

Probee said:

"It is an insidious, crafty, tricky question, brother Damplay. Iniquity itself would not have urged it."

Many old plays included the evil-minded character known as Vice, aka Inequity, aka Wickedness.

Probee concluded:

"It is picking the lock of the scene, not opening it the fair way with a key.

"A play, though it apparel — dress — and present vices in general, flies from all particularities in persons.

"Would you ask of Plautus and Terence, if they lived now, who were Davus [in Terence's *Andria*] or Pseudolus [title character of 'The Liar" in Plautus' play] in the scene?

"Who were Pyrgopolinices [in Plautus' *Miles Gloriosus*, aka *The Braggart Soldier*] or Thraso [in Terence's *Eunuchus*, aka *The Eunuch*]?

"Who were Euclio [in Plautus' *Aulularia*, aka *The Pot of Gold*] or Menedemus [in Terence's *Heutontimorumenos*, aka *The Self-Tormentor*]?"

John Trygust said:

"Yes, he would.

"And he would inquire of Martial, or any other epigrammatist, whom he meant by Titius or Seius — the common John à Noke [John from the Oak] or John à Stile [John from the Stile] —"

These were fictitious names (like John Doe) used in law cases. The fictitious names Gaius Seius and Lucius Titius appear in Roman law.

John Trygust continued:

"— under whom they note all vices and errors taxable to — that can be blamed on — the times! As if there could not be a name for a folly fitted to the stage, but there must be a person found out in nature to own it."

"Why, I can fancy — decide on — a person to myself, boy," Damplay said. "Who shall hinder me?"

John Trygust said:

"And, in not publishing him and making his name known to others, you do no man an injury.

"But if you will utter and make public your own ill meaning on that person under the author's words, you use his comedy to libel someone."

Playwrights could run afoul of libel laws, and so Ben Jonson attempted to make clear that he was not satirizing real individuals, but instead he was satirizing character types.

"Oh, he told us that in a prologue long ago," Damplay said.

Ben Jonson wrote, "They make a libel which he made a play" in the second Prologue to *Epicene, or The Silent Woman*.

"If you do the same reprehensible ill things, still the same reprehension — rebuke — will serve you, though you heard it previously," John Trygust said. "They are his own words. I can invent no better, nor he."

Probee said:

"It is the solemn, humorless vice of interpretation — misinterpretation — that deforms the figure of many a fair scene by drawing it awry, and it is indeed the civil, polite murder of most good plays."

"Drawing it awry" can mean 1) "drawing it badly," or 2) "pulling it out of shape."

Probee continued:

"If I see a thing vively — vividly and clearly — presented on the stage, in such a way that the looking-glass of custom, which is comedy, is so held up to me by the poet that I can therein view the daily examples of men's lives and images of truth in their manners, so drawn for my delight or profit as I may either way use them, then will I — rather than make that true use — hunt out persons to defame by my malice of misapplying?

"And will I imperil the innocence and candor of the author by calumniating him?"

In other words: Suppose that a play vividly presents to me truthful images of men's lives in such a way that I can be entertained or educated by them. Would I then seek to match real people with the characters seen on stage, thereby defaming the real people and putting the playwright in danger of being accused of libel?

Probee continued:

"It is an unjust way of hearing and beholding plays, this, and most unbecoming a gentleman to appear malignantly witty about another's work."

John Trygust said:

"They are no other but narrow and shrunk natures, shriveled up poor things that cannot think well of themselves, who dare to detract and disparage the reputations of others.

"That signature distinctive mark is upon them, and it will last. A half-witted barbarism that no barber's art or his balls will ever expunge or take out!"

One of the barber's arts is bloodletting.

In one of Martial's epigrams appears a man named Cinnamus who is unable to efface the mark of Martial's stigma: Martial's harsh criticism of another man. In another of Martial's epigrams, readers learn that Cinnamus is a barber.

Barber poles are signs that often consist of a red-and-white-swirled pole, capped with a ball on top and at the bottom. The ball at the top represents the basin in which leeches were kept for blood-letting (one of the barber's arts or skills), and the ball at the bottom represented the basin in which blood was collected when a vein was cut in phlebotomy. The pole itself represents the pole that barbers gave patients to squeeze while blood was being collected.

According to the *Oxford English Dictionary*, a ball is "any (approximately) spherical object."

The barber's balls are 1) his round basins, and 2) his balls of soap.

Bloodletting will not expunge the illness of bad interpretation and libel. Nor will soap remove or take out the stain of bad interpretation and libel.

"Barber" also glances at "barbarian."

Damplay said, "Why, boy, this would be a strange empire with an absolute ruler, or rather it would be a tyranny, you would entitle and give your poet a legal right to have, over gentlemen: with the result that they should come to hear and see plays, and say nothing for their money?"

"Oh, yes, say what you will, as long as it is about the matter at hand, to the point, and in its proper place and time," John Trygust said.

"Can anything be out of purpose at a play?" Damplay said. "I see no reason, if I come here and give my eighteen pence or two shillings for my seat, but I should take it out in censure — judgment, good or bad — on the stage."

John Trygust said:

"Your two shillingworth is allowed you, but you will take your ten shillingworth, your twenty shillingworth, and more.

"And you will teach others around you to do the like, who follow your leading face, as if you were to cry up or down — to praise or condemn — every scene by confederacy — unlawful conspiracy — be it right or wrong."

"Who should teach us the right or wrong at a play?" Damplay asked.

John Trygust said:

"If your own science — your own knowledge — cannot do it, or the love of modesty and truth, all other entreaties or attempts — are vain. You are fitter spectators for the bears than us, or for the puppets."

Bear-baitings often occurred in the same theaters in which plays were performed.

Puppet shows were popular.

John Trygust continued:

"This is a popular — a common people's — ignorance indeed, somewhat better appareled — dressed — in you than the people, but a hard-handed and stiff ignorance, worthy a trowel- or a hammer-man, and not only fit to be scorned, but to be triumphed over."

"By whom, boy?" Damplay asked.

John Trygust said:

"By no particular person, but by the general neglect and silence of all.

"Good Master Damplay, be yourself still without a second — without a supporter. Few here are men of your opinion today, I hope; tomorrow, I am sure there will be none, when they have ruminated and thought about this."

Probee said to Damplay, "Let us mind what you have come for, the play, which will draw on to the *epitasis* now."

In the *epitasis*, trials and tribulations ensue and build toward a climax.

CHAPTER 3

— 3.1 —

Tim Item met Master Needle and Nurse Keep. Tim Item was Doctor Rut's apothecary, aka pharmacist. Apothecaries make and sell medicine.

"Where's Master Doctor?" Tim Item asked.

"Oh, Master Tim Item, the doctor's learnèd 'pothecary!" Master Needle said. "You are welcome. He is inside at dinner."

"Dinner? By God's death!" Tim Item said. "To think that he will eat now, having such a business that so concerns him!"

"Why, can any business concern a man like his meat and food?" Master Needle asked.

Tim Item replied, "Oh, twenty million things are more important to a physician who is in practice. I bring him news from all the points of the compass (that's all the parts of the sublunary — under the Moon — globe) of times and double times."

"Times" means "the times." Master Tim Item brings news of the times from various places. "News" includes gossip.

"Double times" may be 1) times filled with deception, or 2) times doubly filled with business, or 3) times doubly filled with news.

Master Needle said, "Go in, in, sweet Item, and furnish forth and provide the table with your news. Deserve and earn your dinner. Sow out your whole bag full. Toss out your items of news as if you were sowing seed. The guests will listen to it."

Tim Item looked toward the dining room and said, "I heard they were fallen out and quarreling."

Master Needle said:

"But they are pieced and put together again."

"Pieced" is a tailor's term. "Piecework" is also known as "Patchwork." In it, small pieces of cloth are sewn together to create a design.

Master Needle continued:

"Their quarrel has been mended and they are at peace. You may go in. You'll find them at high eating."

In other words: They are eating high on the food chain, aka eating luxuriously.

Master Needle continued:

"The parson has an edifying stomach and a persuading palate (like his name)."

An edifying stomach is a stomach that is physically being built up like an edifice, or it is an appetite that is morally edifying.

A persuading palate is a passion for converting others or an appetite that persuades him to eat vast amounts because his taste buds have been persuaded that the food tastes good.

Master Needle continued:

"Parson Palate has begun three draughts of sack — white wine — in doctrines and four in uses."

Doctrines are church dogma or tenets; uses are rituals.

"And they follow him?" Master Item asked.

Master Needle said:

"No, Sir Diaphanous is a recusant in sack. He takes it — alcohol — only in French wine with an allay of water."

A recusant is someone who rejects an item of church dogma. Here Sir Diaphanous Silkworm rejects sack — Spanish white wine — in favor of French wine mixed with water.

Master Needle continued:

"Go in, go in, Item, and stop your peeping."

Tim Item exited.

Nurse Keep said, "I have a month's mind to peep a little, too."

"A month's mind" is a commemorative Catholic Mass held one month after a person's death. Often family members and friends of the deceased shared a meal together. This was a minding day: a day during which one minded — remembered — the dead.

The word "month" also refers to the month after childbirth. The mother was expected to be confined to bed.

Placentia's mother died as a result of giving birth. Her month's mind would have been roughly a month after she gave birth. Nurse Keep would likely have been one of the people observing the month's mind.

The word "peep" has meanings related to 1) looking, and 2) emerging. Revelations about childbirth will emerge in this play, and Nurse Keep will be a part of them.

Master Needle prevented her from peeping at the dinner guests.

Nurse Keep said, "Sweet Mas' [Master] Needle, how are they seated?"

Master Needle said, "At the board's end — head — is My Lady — "

"And my young mistress, Placentia, is by her?" Nurse Keep asked.

Master Needle said:

"Yes. The parson is on the right hand (as he'll not lose his place for thrusting)."

Parson Palate was positioned in such a way that he could easily stab his knife at platters of food and put the stabbed item on his plate.

He also was in the place of honor: the right side of the hostess. No one had been able to thrust him out and take over that spot.

Presumably, dishes of the best kinds of food were close to the host/hostess and the seat of honor.

Master Needle continued:

"And opposite him is Mistress Polish.

"Next, Sir Diaphanous is opposite Sir Moth: The knights were one opposite the other.

"Then the soldier, the man of war, is opposite the man of peace, the lawyer.

"Then the pert doctor is opposite the politic Bias."

"Pert" can mean 1) "skilled," or 2) "ready to express an opinion."

Master Needle continued:

"And Master Compass circumscribes all."

The politic Bias was in the least honored position: the bottom of the table on the left of the hostess.

Compass is at the end of the table, opposite Lady Loadstone and Placentia. He completes the circle, and he has a clear view of everyone.

Compass' position was an anomaly, as seats were usually arranged in a U shape.

Noise came from inside the dinner room.

Running, Pleasance entered the scene and said, "Nurse Keep! Nurse Keep!"

"What noise is that inside?" Master Needle asked.

"Come to my mistress!" Pleasance said to Nurse Keep. "All their weapons are out!"

The word "weapon" can mean "penis."

Nurse Keep said:

"Mischief of men! What evil men are! What day, what hour is this?"

She then said to Master Needle:

"Run for the cellar of strong waters — quickly!"

A cellar is a case of bottles, and strong waters are stimulants, usually containing alcohol.

Master Needle exited.

Pleasance and Nurse Keep exited in the direction of the dining-room.

Compass and Captain Ironside appeared and talked together.

"Were you a madman to do this at the table?" Compass said. "And trouble all the guests, to frighten the ladies and gentlewomen?"

Captain Ironside said:

"A pox upon your women and your half-man there, Court-Sir Ambergris!"

A pox is an illness such as the plague or venereal disease. Smallpox is one example of a plague illness.

Ambergris comes from a whale and is used in perfume.

Of course, Captain Ironside was referring to Sir Diaphanous Silkworm, who was wearing perfume.

Captain Ironside continued:

"A perfumed braggart! He must drink his wine with three parts water, and he must have amber in that, too."

The resin (amber) of some trees was used in medicine.

"And must you therefore break his face with a wine glass and wash his nose in wine?" Compass said.

"Can't he drink in the orthodox, customary manner? Must he have his gums and paynim — pagan — drugs?" Captain Ironside asked.

"Gums" are medicinal resin.

Compass said:

"You should have used the wine glass rather as balance than as the sword of justice, but you have cut his face with it. He bleeds."

Statues of Justice show her carrying a sword and a set of scales. Things that are in balance do not conflict.

Two people drinking wine together need not conflict.

Compass continued:

"Come, you shall take your sanctuary with me. The whole house will be up in arms against you else, within this half-hour. Let's go this way to my lodging."

A place of sanctuary is a place where a person can be safe from arrest.

Compass and Captain Ironside exited.

Doctor Rut, Lady Loadstone, Mistress Polish, and Nurse Keep entered the scene, carrying Placentia over the stage, assisted by Pleasance and Tim Item.

Captain Ironside's violence may have made her ill.

Doctor Rut said:

"A most rude and violent action!"

"Carry Placentia to her bed and use the fricace to her with those oils — massage her with those oils.

"Keep your news, Item, for now, and attend to this business."

Lady Loadstone said to Mistress Polish, "Good gossip, look after her."

"How are you, sweet charge?" Mistress Polish asked Placentia.

A charge is someone to whom one has a duty. Mistress Polish's duty was to help take care of Placentia.

"She's in a sweat," Nurse Keep said.

"Aye, and a faint sweat, by the Virgin Mary!" Mistress Polish said.

Doctor Rut said:

"Let her alone for Tim to treat. He has directions."

Tim Item had the order for and the instructions for making the medicine prescribed for her.

Doctor Rut then said:

"I'll hear your news, Tim Item, when you have done."

Carrying Placentia, Tim Item, Mistress Polish, Nurse Keep, and Pleasance exited.

"Was ever such a guest brought to my table?" Lady Loadstone said.

Doctor Rut said:

"These boisterous soldiers have no better breeding."

Seeing Compass approaching, Doctor Rut said:

"Here Master Compass comes."

Compass entered the scene.

Doctor Rut asked, "Where's your captain, Rudhudibras de Ironside?"

Rud Hudibras was a legendary figure in Britain. He was the son of King Leil, and he founded Carlisle, Canterbury, and Winchester.

His name suggests "Rude Hubris."

Compass answered, "He has gone out of doors."

Mistress Loadstone said:

"That he had never come in them, I may wish.

"He has discredited my house and board with his rude swaggering and blustering manners, and he has endangered my niece's health by drawing his weapon — God knows how far — how dangerously — for Master Doctor does not know."

A "weapon" can be a penis, and such a weapon can put a virgin maiden in danger of no longer being a virgin maiden.

Compass said, "The doctor is an ass then if he says so, and if he cannot with his conjuring names, Hippocrates, Galen, or Rasis, Avicen, Averroes, cure a poor wench's falling in a swoon and fainting, which a poor farthing exchanged for *rosa solis* or cinnamon water would."

"A poor farthing exchanged for *rosa solis*" is a farthing's worth of the cure for fainting called *rosa solis.*

Rosa solis means "rose of the sun." It was a medicinal drink made from the sundew plant (drosera).

The names to conjure by were those of famous doctors and authors.

Hippocrates (460-370 B.C.E.) and Galen (129-216 B.C.E.) were ancient Greek physicians.

Rasis (865?-935? C.E.) was a ninth-century Arabian physician.

Avicenna (980-1037 C.E.) was a Persian physician.

Averroes (1126-1198 C.E.) wrote about medicine and translated Aristotle.

Nurse Keep and Mistress Polish entered the scene.

Lady Loadstone said, "What is the news now? How is she doing?"

"She's somewhat better," Nurse Keep said. "Master Item has brought her a little about. She is recovering a little."

Mistress Polish said:

"But there's Sir Moth, your brother, who has fallen into a fit of the happyplex.

"It would be a happy place for him and us if he could steal to heaven thus."

By "happyplex," Mistress Polish meant "apoplexy," aka stroke.

In other words: If Sir Moth Interest were in heaven, it would be a happy place for him. It would also make Mistress Polish and Placentia happy.

Mistress Polish continued:

"All in the house are calling 'Master Doctor! Master Doctor!'

"The parson, he has given Sir Moth Interest gone — considered him dead — this half-hour.

"He's pale in the mouth already for the fear of the fierce captain."

Doctor Rut exited.

Lady Loadstone said:

"Help me to my chamber, Nurse Keep.

"I wish that I could see the day no more, and instead that night hung over me like some dark cloud so that, buried with this loss of my good name, I and my house might perish, thus forgotten."

Lady Loadstone, Nurse Keep, and Mistress Polish exited.

"Her taking it to heart thus more afflicts me than all these accidents and incidents, for they'll blow over and pass on," Compass said.

Master Practice and Sir Diaphanous Silkworm entered the scene.

Master Practice said:

"It was a barbarous injury, I confess, but if you will be counseled and advised, sir, by me, the reverend, worthy-of-respect law lies open to repair your reputation. That will give you damages: I have known five thousand pounds to be given in court for a finger.

"And let me pack your jury. I will find jurors who will be partial toward you and your case."

Sir Diaphanous Silkworm said, "There's nothing that vexes me except that he has stained my new white satin doublet, and bespattered my spick and span silk stockings, on the day they were first put on," Sir Diaphanous Silkworm said. "And here's a spot on my hose, too."

Hose cover the thighs and loins.

"Shrewd maims! Grievous injuries!" Compass said. "Your clothes are wounded desperately, and that, I think, troubles a courtier more, an exact, refined courtier, than a gash in his flesh."

"My flesh?" Sir Diaphanous Silkworm said. "I swear, had he given me twice so much hurt, I never should have reckoned it — I would not have regarded it as worthy of comment. But my clothes to be defaced and stigmatized — marked with a stain — so foully! I take it as a contumely — an insult — done me above the wisdom of our laws to correct and put right."

If the law won't right wrongs, one can take matters into one's own hands.

Compass said, "Why then, you'll challenge him? You'll formally challenge him to duel in a written letter?"

"I will take thought," Sir Diaphanous Silkworm said, "though Master Practice here does urge the law and the creditable reputation for honor it will give me, besides great damages — let him pack my jury."

Compass said to himself:

"He speaks like Master Practice, one who is the child of a profession he's vowed and devoted to and servant to the study he has taken, a 'pure and uncorrupted' apprentice at law!"

He then said out loud:

"But you must have the counsel of the sword, and you must square your action to their canons and that brotherhood if you do right. You must follow the canons — the rules — of dueling."

"The counsel of the sword" is advice from someone who has settled an argument by dueling.

Master Practice said:

"I tell you, Master Compass, that you don't speak like a friend to the laws, nor even a subject to the laws, to persuade him thus to the breach of the peace.

"Sir, you forget that there is a court above, that of the Star Chamber, to punish routs and riots."

Dueling was against the law.

Compass replied:

"No, young master, although your name is Practice there in term time when the courts are open, I do remember it.

"But you'll not hear what I was bound to say, but, like a wild young haggard — untrained — justice, you will fly at and attack and breach the peace before you know whether the amorous knight dares to break the peace of conscience in a duel."

A haggard is an untrained bird of prey that could fly at and attack something prematurely.

Amorous knights appeared in romances; Sir Diaphanous Silkworm was courting Placentia.

The "peace of conscience" could mean that Sir Diaphanous Silkworm is a conscientious objector to violence.

Sir Diaphanous Silkworm said, "Truly, Master Compass, I take you to be my friend and ask you to be my second — my assistant — in the duel. You shall settle for me any matter that's reasonable, as long as we may meet fairly on even terms."

"We" meant Captain Ironside and Sir Diaphanous Silkworm.

Compass said:

"I shall persuade — urge — no otherwise. And you shall take your learnèd counsel, Master Practice, to advise you. I'll run and go along with him.

"You say you'll meet him — Captain Ironside — on even terms."

The duel will not be even. The odds for each duelist would not be even.

Compass then gave reasons why the duel could not be even:

"I do not see indeed how the duel can be even, between Ironside and you, now I consider it.

"He is my brother, I do confess — we have called each other 'brother' for twenty years — but you are, sir, a knight in court, with allies there, and you are so befriended, that you may easily answer the worst outcome."

The worst outcome would be death. If Captain Ironside were to die in the duel, Sir Diaphanous Silkworm would be able to pay the probable fine that would result.

Advantage: Sir Diaphanous Silkworm.

But if Sir Diaphanous Silkworm were to die in the duel, that would be another kind of worst outcome; still, he could answer that, too — it would be easy for him to die in the duel. That would be his answer to the duel.

Advantage: Captain Ironside.

Compass continued:

"He is a known, noted, bold boy of the sword, and he has all men's eyes upon him. And there's no London jury but are led in evidence as far by common fame and reputation as they are by present deposition."

According to Compass, London juries were swayed more by the reputation of and gossip about those involved in lawsuits than they were by evidence and testimony.

Captain Ironside has a reputation as a military man, and London juries are swayed by reputations.

Advantage: Captain Ironside.

Compass continued:

"Then you have many brethren and near kinsmen. If he should kill you, it will be a lasting quarrel between them and him."

Captain Ironside may well kill Sir Diaphanous Silkworm.

Advantage: Captain Ironside.

But Sir Diaphanous Silkworm has many brethren and near kinsmen who will avenge him against this one captain.

Advantage: Sir Diaphanous Silkworm.

Compass continued:

"Whereas Rud Ironside, although he has got his head into a beaver with a huge feather, is just a currier's son, and he has not two old Cordovan skins to leave in leather caps for others to mourn him in — to wear as a sign of mourning — if he should die."

Rud Ironside is Rudhudibras de Ironside, the name Doctor Rut had given to Captain Ironside.

A beaver is the visor of a helmet; the feather was a decoration for the helmet.

A currier colors leather after it is cured. Curing removes water from the hide.

"Cordovan skins" is leather from Cordoba, Spain.

Captain Ironside can leave little behind for his survivors: people who will mourn him if Sir Diaphanous Silkworm. should kill him. Sir Diaphanous Silkworm will leave much behind.

Advantage: Sir Diaphanous Silkworm.

Compass continued:

"Again, you are generally beloved, he hated so much, so that all the hearts and votes — prayers — of men go with you in the wishing all prosperity to your purpose."

Advantage: Sir Diaphanous Silkworm.

Of course, as an experienced soldier, Captain Ironside has a huge advantage over the not-at-all experienced Sir Diaphanous Silkworm.

Advantage: Captain Ironside.

Compass then gave an equivocal speech. His words for each argument could be taken either to say that Captain Ironside was favored to win the duel, or to say that Sir Diaphanous was favored to win the duel.

Compass said:

"Captain Ironside is a fat, corpulent, unwieldy fellow."

The adjectives "fat," "corpulent," and "unwieldy" have a negative sense in which the person they are applied to is excessively heavy, out of shape, uncoordinated, and unable to move well.

Point: Captain Ironside is fat and out of shape.

Advantage: Sir Diaphanous Silkworm.

In this society, however. the adjectives "fat," "corpulent," and "unwieldy" also have positive meanings as well as the usual negative. The adjectives can mean "big-bodied" and "muscular" and "difficult to move." The word "fat" can mean "well fed." (In some cultures, being plump is regarded as something good.) "Corpulent" can mean "massive." Also, Captain Ironside is unwieldy: No one can push him around.

Point: Captain Ironside is well fed, massive, and hard to push around.

Advantage: Captain Ironside.

Compass continued:

"In contrast, you are a dieted spark, fit for the combat."

"A dieted spark" can mean a spirited man who is not overweight or obese, someone who is ready to fight well.

Advantage: Sir Diaphanous Silkworm.

A "dieted spark" can also mean a thin man with a fine figure. Sir Diaphanous Silkworm's "fine figure" is likely to be due to his splendid clothing rather than hours spent in exercise. His fitness can mean that his clothing fits well, not that he is physically fit.

Advantage: Captain Ironside.

Compass continued:

"Captain Ironside has killed so many that it is ten to one his turn is next."

According to this incorrect use of statistics and probability, Captain Ironside is likely to die in this fight.

Advantage: Sir Diaphanous Silkworm.

Compass continued:

"You never fought with any, much less slew any, and therefore you have the hopes before you."

According to this incorrect use of statistics and probability, Sir Diaphanous Silkworm is likely to defeat Captain Ironside.

Advantage: Sir Diaphanous Silkworm.

Of course, as an experienced soldier, Captain Ironside has a huge advantage over the not-at-all experienced Sir Diaphanous Silkworm; however, Captain Ironside has said that lesser men sometimes defeat men of valor.

Advantage: Captain Ironside, but with a reservation.

Compass continued:

"I hope these things thus specified to you are fair advantages: You cannot encounter him upon equal terms.

"Besides, Sir Silkworm, he has done you wrong in a most high degree, and sense of such an injury received should so exacuate — sharpen — and whet your choler that you should count yourself a host — an army — of men compared to him.

"And therefore you, brave sir, have no more reason to provoke or challenge him than the huge great porter has to try his strength upon an infant."

King Charles I had a porter named William Evans who was reputed to be over seven feet tall.

If Sir Diaphanous Silkworm's anger made him think that he was the equivalent of an entire army, he had no need to fight Captain Ironside. It was already certain that he would win.

Advantage: Sir Diaphanous Silkworm.

But in history, the huge porter — William Evans (d. 1636) — was not physically fit and healthy. If the army was metaphorically like the huge porter, the army was not powerful. Victory was not sure, after all.

Advantage: Captain Ironside.

Sir Diaphanous Silkworm said, "Master Compass, you rather spur me on than in any way abate and reduce my courage to the enterprise."

According to his words, he was all the more eager to fight Captain Ironside after hearing Compass' words.

Compass said:

"All counsel's as it's taken: All advice is what you make of it."

This is true: Compass' advice could be taken as encouragement to fight the duel, or as discouragement to fight the duel.

Compass continued:

"If you stand on point of honor not to have any odds, I have rather dissuaded you than otherwise."

In other words: If as a point of honor, you wish to duel on even terms and not have anything to give you an advantage, I have given you reasons not to duel. I have given you reasons to think you will lose.

Compass continued:

"If you wish to duel upon terms of humor and revenge, I have encouraged you."

In other words: If you wish to duel because of your temperament and a desire for revenge, I have given you reasons to think you will win.

Compass continued:

"So that I think that I have done the part of a friend on either side: In furnishing your fear with a basis for it first, if you have any; or, if you dare to fight, to heighten and confirm your resolution and determination to persist."

"I now do crave your pardon, Master Compass," Master Practice said. "I did not apprehend and understand your way before, the true perimeter and scope of it: You have circles and such fine draughts about!"

Master Practice was praising the thoroughness of Compass' logic.

The *perimeter* is the circumference.

The *scope* is what is covered.

The *circle* is the figure of the circumference.

The *draughts* outline or plot the figure. They are drawn around the figure to define it.

In other words: Anyone who understands geometry has the intellectual power to speak rationally, as you have just shown.

Sir Diaphanous Silkworm said:

"Sir, I do thank you, I thank you, Master Compass, heartily.

"I must confess I have never fought before, and I'll be glad to do things orderly, in the right place.

"I ask you to instruct me.

"Is it best to fight ambitiously or maliciously?"

A person ambitious to get a good reputation for honor would fight fairly. A person whose only objective is to win would fight dirty.

"Sir, if you never fought before, be wary," Compass said. "Don't trust yourself too much. Don't be overconfident."

"Why?" Sir Diaphanous Silkworm asked. "I assure you I'm very angry."

Compass said:

"Do not allow, though, the flatuous [flatulent], windy choler — anger — of your heart to move the clapper — tongue — of your understanding, which is the guiding faculty: your reason.

"You don't know if you'll fight or not, once you are brought to the place of the duel."

In other words: Don't allow your anger to make you burst out in an angry speech made without the use of your reason. Don't be like a bell that clangs in a high wind rather than a bell-ringer who makes harmonious music.

Sir Diaphanous Silkworm said, "Oh, yes, I have imagined him trebled-armed, provoked, too, and as furious as Homer makes Achilles; and I find that I am not frightened by his reputation one tiny jot."

"Treble-armed" can mean 1) with three arms, or 2) with three different kinds of weapons.

In Achilles' *Iliad*, Achilles first argues with Agamemnon, and later, after Hector kills Achilles' friend Patroclus, Achilles becomes furious at Hector.

Compass said:

"Well, yet take heed. These imaginary fights are less than skirmishes, the fight of shadows:

"For shadows have their figure, motion, and their umbratile — shadowy — action from the real physical posture and motion of the body's act. Whereas imaginarily many times those men may fight, yet in reality they scarcely dare eye one another, much less meet."

In other words: Men may imagine many times fighting each other, but when they actually meet in a duel, they scarcely dare to look at each other, much less fight.

Compass continued:

"But if there is no help for it and no stopping the duel, in faith, I would wish you to send him a fair challenge."

"I will go pen it immediately," Sir Diaphanous Silkworm said.

"But word it in the most high-minded, generous terms," Compass said.

"Let me alone," Sir Diaphanous Silkworm said. "Leave it to me."

"And word it with silken phrase: Make it the courtliest kind of quarrel," Master Practice said.

Sir Diaphanous Silkworm exited.

"He'll make it a petition for his peace," Compass said.

In other words: Instead of fighting, he'll get a legal bond to maintain peace between Captain Ironside and him. Or, possibly, his letter would ask for a peaceful resolution to their dispute; it need not be a request that the two meet in a duel.

"Oh, yes, of right, and he may do it by law," Master Practice said.

In other words: His doing so is right and justified, as long as he follows the law.

Doctor Rut, Parson Palate, and Master Bias brought out Sir Moth Interest, who was in a chair. Tim Item and Mistress Polish followed them.

Doctor Rut said:

"Come, bring him out into the air a little. Set him down there. Bend him; yet bend him more."

Parson Palate and Master Bias attempted to bend Sir Moth Interest's head to his knees.

Doctor Rut continued:

"Dash that glass of water in his face."

Parson Palate splashed Sir Moth Interest's face with water.

Doctor Rut continued:

"Now tweak him by the nose."

Master Bias pulled Sir Moth Interest's nose.

Doctor Rut continued:

"Hard, harder still. If it just calls the blood up from the heart, I ask no more.

"See what a fear can do!"

Sir Moth Interest was afraid of Captain Ironside. That fear had caused him to fall into this condition.

Master Bias pulled Sir Moth Interest's nose harder.

Doctor Rut continued:

"Pinch him in the nape of the neck now."

Tim Item hesitated.

Doctor Rut continued:

"Nip him! Nip him!"

He demonstrated, pinching Sir Moth Interest, who startled.

"He feels the pinch," Tim Item said. "There's life in him."

"He groans and stirs," Parson Palate said.

"Tell him the captain's gone," Doctor Rut said.

Captain Ironside had left the vicinity.

Sir Moth Interest said, "Huh!"

"The captain's gone, sir," Master Palate said to Sir Moth Interest.

"Give him a box — hard! hard! — on his left ear," Doctor Rut said.

No one moved.

Doctor Rut struck Sir Moth Interest on his ear.

"Ow!" Sir Moth Interest said.

"How do you feel?" Doctor Rut asked.

"Sore! Sore!" Sir Moth Interest said.

"But where?" Doctor Rut asked.

"In my neck," Sir Moth Interest said.

"I nipped him there," Doctor Rut said to the others.

"And in my head," Sir Moth Interest said.

"I boxed him twice or thrice to move those sinews," Doctor Rut said.

"Sinews" are muscles.

"I swear you did," Master Bias said.

"What a brave — excellent — man is a doctor, to beat one into health!" Mistress Polish said. "I thought his blows would even have killed him. Sir Moth Interest did feel no more than a great horse."

"Is the wild captain gone, that man of murder?" Sir Moth Interest asked.

"All is calm and quiet," Master Bias said.

"Do you say so, Cousin Bias?" Sir Moth Interest said. "Then all's well."

The word "cousin" indicates kinship. Master Bias had not yet married Placentia, but Sir Moth Interest was firmly convinced that Master Bias would marry her.

"How quickly a man is lost!" Parson Palate said.

"And soon recovered!" Master Bias said.

Mistress Polish said, "Where there are means and doctors, learnèd men and their apothecaries, who are not now, as Chaucer says, their friendship to begin, well could they teach each other how to win [cure people] in their swath-bands —"

Chaucer, Gen. Prol., 428 wrote, "*Hir frendship was nought newe to biginne.*" Ben Jonson interpreted "newe" to mean "now."

Doctor Rut and apothecary Tim Item had long been friends. Because of their long working together, they could effect cures. By being friends and working together, they would long have been learning the art of medicine.

"Swath-bands" are swaddling bands. They are also bandages.

Doctor Rut interrupted, "— stop your poetry, good gossip, stop your Chaucer's clouts, and wash your dishes with them. We must rub up — uproot

— the roots of his disease, and so we request your silence for a while, or else your absence."

"Clouts" are 1) swaddling-cloths, aka a baby's garments, including cloth diapers, or 2) rags.

"Nay, I know when to hold my peace," Mistress Polish said.

Doctor Rut said to her:

"Then do it."

He then said:

"Give me your hand, Sir Moth. Let's feel your pulse."

He felt Sir Moth Interest's pulse and said:

"It is a pursiness, a kind of stoppage or obstruction, or tumor of the purse, for want of exercise, that you are troubled with."

"Pursiness" is "shortness of breath." Of course, the word glances at the word "purse," aka moneybag. One illness afflicting Sir Moth Interest is greed: an excessive love of money. The other illness is shortness of breath due to his fear of Captain Ironside.

A tumor is a swelling. A purse is a bag. A medical example of a swelling of the purse could be swollen testicles, but in Sir Moth Interest's case, he suffers from a swollen moneybag. The obstruction was too-tight purse-strings.

Doctor Rut continued:

"You have some ligatures in the neck of your *vesica* or *marsupium* that are so close-knit that you cannot evaporate, and therefore you must use relaxatives."

"Ligatures" can be 1) ligaments, or 2) purse-strings.

A *vesica* is a bladder, and a *marsupium* is a pouch.

"Close-knit" means close-tied or tightly tied.

Sir Moth Interest's moneybag is too full and too tightly tied, and it never gets exercise. His moneybag needs to be opened so that some of the coins can "evaporate" into general circulation. Sir Moth Interest is tight-fisted, and relaxatives — muscle relaxants — would help open his hand.

Doctor Rut said:

"Besides, they say you have grown so restive that you cannot except with trouble put your hand into your pocket to discharge a reckoning, and this we sons of physic do call *chiragra*, a kind of cramp or hand-gout. You shall purge for it."

"Restive" can mean 1) inactive, or 2) stubborn.

Sir Moth Interest's hand cannot reach into his pocket and take out money to discharge — pay — a reckoning, aka bill.

To correct this problem, Sir Moth Interest needs to be purged of some of his money. If he becomes more willing to spend money, his hand will more easily go into his pocket to pull out coins. His hand will no longer have the hand-gout, aka *chiragra.*

A medical kind of purge is vomiting or defecation.

Tim Item said, "Indeed, Your Worship should do well to advise him to cleanse his body all the three high ways: that is, by sweat, purge, and phlebotomy."

Sweat, purge, and phlebotomy were means of medical cures. Patients would be made to sweat, to vomit or defecate, and/or to bleed.

Doctor Rut said:

"You say well, learnèd Tim. I'll first prescribe him to give his purse a purge once, twice a week at dice or cards.

"And when the weather is open, sweat at a bowling alley, or be let blood in the lending vein, and bleed a matter of fifty or threescore ounces at a time."

Sir Moth Interest needs to purge some of his money. He can do that by losing at dice or cards.

Losing money while betting on the game of bowls will make him sweat or vomit.

The "lending vein" is the frame of mind that would allow Sir Moth Interest to lend money, presumably not at usurious rates.

The important point is that Sir Moth Interest needs to bleed money.

Doctor Rut continued:

"Then put your thumbs under your girdle — your belt — and have somebody else pull out your purse for you, until with more ease and a good habit — custom or habitual practice — you can do it yourself.

"And then be sure always to keep a good diet, and have your table furnished from one end to the other: It is good for the eyes, but feed yourself on one dish still."

In other words, have guests at meals and spend money to feed them well.

Doctor Rut continued:

"Have your diet-drink — your nutritional drink — habitually ready in bottles, which must come from the King's Head Tavern on Fish Street Hill."

In other words: Spend money on good strong ale. It will build up your constitution (and reduce the weight of your moneybag).

Doctor Rut continued:

"I will prescribe you nothing but what I'll take before you my own self. That is my course with all my patients."

Food and drink are some good things for Sir Moth Interest to spend his money on.

Doctor Rut followed his own advice about diet, and he was willing to help Sir Moth eat some of the food and drink some of the ale.

Doctor Rut said that he would take it before Sir Moth Interest. This can mean 1) He would follow his own nutritional advice before prescribing it for Sir Moth, 2) He would be Sir Moth's food-taster, eating some of the food before Sir Moth ate it to make sure it was not poisoned, and/or 3) He would eat the food in front of Sir Moth, at Sir Moth's table.

"Very methodical, *secundum artem* — according to the art," Parson Palate said.

"And very safe *pro captu recipientis* — for the pleasing of the recipient," Master Bias said.

"All errant learnèd men, how they 'spute Latin!" Mistress Palate said.

By "errant" (wrong-headed), Mistress Polish meant "arrant" (learned).

By "'spute," Mistress Polish meant "dispute," but "to spew" means "to vomit."

Doctor Rut said, "I learned this prescription from a Jew, and a great rabbi, who every morning mixed his cup of white wine with sugar and, by the residence — residue — in the bottom, would make report of any chronic, lasting malady, such as Sir Moth's is, being an oppilation — an obstruction — in that which you call the neck of the money bladder, most anatomical and by dissection."

The rabbi's report was "most anatomical and by dissection." These were words that Doctor Rut used to show approval.

Chances are that the rabbi looked at the wine after it had passed through his bladder. Doctors then and now look at urine to help determine a patient's health. Urine should be clear, and cloudy urine can indicate a medical problem.

The rabbi suffered from the same disease as Sir Moth Interest.

Nurse Keep entered the scene and said, "Oh, Master Doctor, and his 'pothecary, good Master Item, and my Mistress Polish! We need you all above! She's fallen again into a worse fit than ever."

"Who?" Mistress Polish asked.

"Your charge," Nurse Keep answered.

Placentia was ill again.

"Come away, gentlemen," Mistress Polish said.

Mistress Polish, Nurse Keep, Parson Palate, Doctor Rut, and Tim Item exited.

Sir Moth Interest said, "This fit — this session — with the doctor has mended — cured — me past expectation."

He exited, leaving Master Bias behind, alone.

Compass, Sir Diaphanous Silkworm, and Master Practice entered the scene. Sir Diaphanous Silkworm was holding a letter.

"Oh, Sir Diaphanous, have you finished your letter?" Compass asked.

"I have brought it," Sir Diaphanous Silkworm said.

"That's well," Master Practice said.

"But who shall carry it now?" Compass asked.

"A friend," Sir Diaphanous Silkworm said. "I'll find a friend to carry it. Master Bias here will not deny me my request."

"What request is it?" Master Bias asked.

"To carry a challenge I have written to Captain Ironside," Sir Diaphanous Silkworm answered.

Master Bias said:

"By my faith, but I will deny you your request, sir; you shall pardon me.

"For a twi-reason — a double reason — of state, I'll bear no challenges: I will not hazard my lord's favor so or forfeit my own judgment with His Honor by turning into a ruffian."

He would not risk his lord's favor, and he would not give up the reputation he had with his lord.

Dueling was against the law, and carrying a challenge to duel to another person was against the law. If Master Bias were to do that, he would be a ruffian.

Master Bias continued:

"I have to commend me nothing except His Lordship's good opinion, and in addition to it my calligraphy, a beautiful handwriting fit for a secretary — a professional writer."

Secretaries used different kinds of styles of handwriting for different kinds of documents. One style was called the secretary hand.

Master Bias continued:

"Now you know a man's hand, being his executing part in fight, is more obnoxious to — that is, more liable to be affected by — the common peril —"

Duelists use their hands to control their weapons, and so their hands were liable to be injured.

Sir Diaphanous Silkworm interrupted, "— you shall not fight, sir; you shall only find my antagonist and commit us fairly there upon the ground on equal terms."

Master Bias would not fight, but he would have to find Captain Ironside, deliver the letter, and find a dueling ground that would be fair to both duelists and that both duelists would commit to.

"Oh, sir!" Master Bias said. "But if my lord should hear I stood at the end — participated in even a minor way — of any quarrel, it would be an end of me in a political career in state affairs. I have read the political writers, and I have heard the opinions of our best divines."

In 1613, King James I made into law his *Edict and Severe Censure against Private Combats and Combatants*. Duelists and their seconds (supporters) and those who carried challenges would be banished from court for seven years. Master Bias, of course, wanted a career at court.

Divines would presumably be against dueling and the killing it causes.

Exodus 20:13 states, "*Thou shalt not kill*" (King James Version).

"The gentleman has reason," Compass said. "Where was first the birth of your acquaintance, or the cradle of your strict friendship made?"

"We met in France, sir," Sir Diaphanous Silkworm answered.

Compass said:

"In France, that garden of humanity and mental cultivation, the very seed-plot — seeding ground — of all courtesies!

"I marvel that your friendship sucked that aliment and nourishment, the milk of France, and see this sour effect it does produce in contrast to all the sweet benefits of travel.

"There, every gentleman professing to be skilled in arms thinks that he is bound in honor to embrace and welcome the bearing of a challenge for another without either questioning the cause or asking the least color — pretext or show — of reason.

"There's no cowardice and no poltroonery such as urging 'why?' and ' wherefore?'

"Instead, there is only this: Carry a challenge, die, and do the thing."

A poltroon is a complete and utter coward.

France was (and is) a country of intellectual cultivation, and yet many gentlemen died in duels there.

Master Bias said out loud:

"Why, listen, Master Compass, I just desire to speak in your ear in private."

He then said quietly to him:

"I would carry his challenge, if I only hoped your Captain Ironside was angry enough to kill him.

"For, to tell you the truth, this knight — Sir Diaphanous — is an impertinent, meddlesome person in court, we think, and he troubles my lord's lodgings and his table with frequent and unnecessary visits, which we (the better sort of followers) don't like, being his fellow equals in all other places except our master's table, and we disdain to do those servile, unworthy-of-a-gentleman services that often his foolish pride and empire — that is, his tyranny — will exact against the heart or humor of a gentleman."

Compass replied:

"In truth, Master Bias, I'd not have you think that I speak to flatter you, but you are one of the deepest politicians I ever met, and the most subtly rational. I admire you."

In this context, a politician is a schemer. Does Compass admire him?

The word "subtle" can mean crafty and cunning.

Reason can be used for good or for evil.

The word "admire" can mean "marvel at." Compass marvels that someone like Master Bias can exist.

Compass continued:

"But don't you believe in such a case that you are an accessory to his death, an accessory because you carry a challenge from him with such a purpose and intention?"

That purpose, of course, was to get Sir Diaphanous Silkworm killed. Master Bias would be an accessory before the fact: He would help arrange things so that Captain Ironside could kill Sir Diaphanous Silkworm.

Bias said:

"Sir, the corruption of one thing in nature is held the generation of another."

Dead things became fertilizer to grow living things.

A proverb stated, "The corruption of one is the generation of another."

Bias continued:

"And therefore I had rather be accessory to his death than to his life."

"A new moral philosophy, too!" Compass said. "You'll carry the challenge then?"

An old moral philosophy stated, "Thou shalt not kill."

"I would if I were sure that it would not incense and inflame Captain Ironside's choler — his anger — and make him want to beat the messenger," Master Bias said.

"Oh, I'll secure you and keep you safe," Compass said. "You shall deliver the letter to Captain Ironside in my lodging safely and do your friend Sir Diaphanous a service worthy of his thanks."

"I'll venture it, upon so good induction — inducement — in order to rid the court of an impediment, this baggage — worthless — knight," Bias said.

Impedimenta is Latin for the baggage of an army.

Captain Ironside entered the scene.

He said:

"Peace to you all, gentlemen, except to this upstart mushroom, who I hear is menacing me with a challenge, which I come to anticipate and save the law a labor."

Upstarts are mushrooms because mushrooms spring up overnight, as upstart social climbers seem to do. Captain Ironside was calling Sir Diaphanous Silkworm a mushroom, but since Sir Diaphanous is a knight, the insult is undeserved except that Sir Diaphanous Silkworm is instigating the duel as a way to gain credit for reputation and so rise in society.

By having the duel now, they would save the law the trouble of trying to prevent it.

Captain Ironside said to Sir Diaphanous Silkworm, "Will you fight, sir?"

"Yes, in my shirt," Sir Diaphanous Silkworm said.

He took off his doublet: a kind of jacket.

"Oh, that's to save your doublet," Captain Ironside said. "I know it is a court trick! You would rather have an ulcer — a running sore — in your body than an additional pink in your clothes."

A pink is a decorative hole in clothing. The colorful cloth underneath shows through it.

A pink is also a sword's or dagger's stab.

"Captain, you are a coward if you do not fight in your shirt," Sir Diaphanous Silkworm said.

He drew his sword.

Captain Ironside said:

"Sir, I do not intend to delay the fight because you say that, nor do I intend yet to take off my doublet."

Of course he would not delay the fight: Sir Diaphanous Silkworm had just called him a coward.

He drew his sword.

Captain Ironside continued:

"You've now a reason to call me coward: because I won't fight in my shirt, I who fear more the touch of the common and life-giving air than all your fury and the panoply — the full suit of armor."

"Which is at best but a thin linen armor," Master Practice said. "I think a cup of generous, good-quality wine would be better than fighting in your shirts."

"Sir, sir, my valor is a valor of another nature than to be mended by a cup of wine," Sir Diaphanous Silkworm said.

"I would be glad to hear of any different kinds of valors," Compass said. "I am one who has known hitherto only the one virtue that they call fortitude to be worthy of the name of valor."

Valor is fortitude: courage.

"Anyone who has not fortitude is justly thought to be a coward," Captain Ironside said. "And he — Sir Diaphanous — is such a coward."

"Oh, you have read the play there, *The New Inn* of Ben Jonson's, that decries and openly condemns all other valor but what is for the public," Sir Diaphanous Silkworm said.

In Act 4, Scene 4 of Ben Jonson's play *The New Inn*, the character Lovell discusses and defends true valor. He says that true valor is a true science of distinguishing what's good or evil. It springs out of reason and tends to perfect honor; the end goal of true valor is always honor and the public good. He also says that an act is not valorous if it is done for a private cause or reason.

"I think that, too," Captain Ironside said. "But I did not learn it there. I think no valor exists for a private cause or reason."

"Sir, I'll redargue — confute or challenge — you by disputation and argument," Sir Diaphanous Silkworm said.

"Oh, let's hear this!" Compass said. "I long to hear a man dispute in his shirt about valor, and his sword drawn in his hand."

Master Practice said, "Sir Diaphanous' valor will catch a cold."

Both Compass and Master Practice would mock the various kinds of valor that Sir Diaphanous Silkworm would talk about.

Master Practice then said to Sir Diaphanous, "Put on your doublet."

Compass said quietly to Master Practice:

"His valor will remain cold — he will stay calm — you are deceived, and it will relish — please — much the sweeter in our ears.

"It may be, too, in the ordinance of nature — the way nature orders things that their valors are not yet so combative or truly antagonistic as to fight but may admit to hear about some divisions — different kinds — of fortitude that may put them off their quarrel."

Sir Diaphanous Silkworm said:

"I would have no man think me so ungoverned or subject to my passion — strong feeling — but I can deliver him a lecture between my undertakings and executions."

This can mean 1) "in the time between my undertaking to fight a duel and my execution — actually doing — my undertaking," or 2) "between what I say I will do and what I actually do."

Sir Diaphanous Silkworm continued:

"I know all kinds of doing the business that the town calls valor."

Compass said quietly to Master Practice, "Yes, he has read the town. Towntop's his author!"

In other words: Sir Diaphanous Silkworm has studied the attitude of Londoners, and he has listened to gossip as people whipped the parish-top and made it spin. That is where he has gained his ideas about valor.

Towntop, aka parish-top, is a large whipping-top that provided entertainment and exercise for people in a community.

Compass asked Sir Diaphanous Silkworm out loud, "What is your first kind of valor?"

"First is a rash headlong unexperience — valor arising from lack of experience," Sir Diaphanous Silkworm said.

The First Kind of Valor: People can show courage by recklessly rushing into danger without knowing how dangerous the situation is.

Compass said, "Which is in children, fools, or your street gallants of the first head."

'Of the first head" means "superior to others." Compass was being sarcastic.

"A pretty kind of valor!" Master Practice said.

Compass said quietly to Master Practice, "Commend him; he will spin it out in his shirt as fine and flimsy as the thread in that shirt of his."

"The next is an indiscreet presumption, grounded upon frequent escapes," Sir Diaphanous Silkworm said.

The Second Kind of Valor: People can show valor because they are very confident of being able to escape from a dangerous situation.

Compass said:

"Or the insufficiency — the lack — of adversaries, and this is in your common fighting brothers, your old perdus — sentinels at an outpost — who, after a time, do think, the one, that they are shot-free, the other, that they are sword-free."

These are sentinels who have been placed at dangerous outposts, but the battle has moved away from them and they are beyond the reach of bullets and swords and therefore they are safe. Such sentinels can feel valorous.

Compass then asked Sir Diaphanous Silkworm, "What is your third kind of valor?"

He replied, "It is nothing but an excess of choler that reigns in testy, grumpy old men —"

The Third Kind of Valor: An excess of anger displayed by testy, grumpy old men. Such old men can threaten and bluster.

Compass interrupted, "Noblemen's porters and self-conceited poets who think too highly of themselves."

"And is rather a peevishness than any part of valor," Sir Diaphanous Silkworm said.

Master Practice said quietly to Compass, "He but rehearses; he concludes no valor."

In other words: Sir Diaphanous Silkworm talks about valor, but he has not described anything that is true valor.

Compass replied quietly to Master Practice, "His harangue — lecture — undertakes a history of distempers — incidents of angry people — as they are practiced, and no more."

He then asked Sir Diaphanous Silkworm, "Your next form of valor?"

Sir Diaphanous Silkworm began, "It is a dull desperate resolving —"

Compass interrupted, "— in case of some necessitous, impoverished misery, or incumbent — threatening — evil."

Master Practice said, "Narrowness of mind, or ignorance being the root of it."

Sir Diaphanous Silkworm finished his sentence, "— which you shall find in gamesters quite blown up."

The Fourth Kind of Valor: People who have been ruined by gambling or who are in some other desperate situation can resolve to do something desperate.

"Bankrupt merchants, undiscovered and still-hidden traitors," Compass said.

People who are desperate can rebel against their government.

Master Practice said, "Or your exemplified malefactors — criminals who have been made an example to others and have survived their infamy and punishment."

Compass said:

"For example, one who has lost his ears by a just sentence of the Star Chamber, a right valiant knave.

"And is a histrionical contempt of what a man fears most, it being an evil in his own apprehension unavoidable."

If it is histrionical, then it is theatrically extravagant and hypocritical.

"Contempt of what a man fears most" is "disrespect to one's sovereign," whether secular or divine.

One kind of apprehension is being arrested.

Master Practice said, "This kind of valor is found in cowards wounded mortally, or thieves adjudged — sentenced — to die."

Compass said, "This is a valor that I should desire much to see encouraged, as being a special entertainment for our rogue people who are spectators at an execution, and it does make often good sport to them from the gallows to the ground."

The people who are being executed could die with some valor by accepting their fate and by repenting their sins. Such a display of valor and repentance would entertain and benefit the spectators from the time the criminals stepped on the gallows to the time when their bodies were taken from the rope and laid on the ground to be quartered.

This English punishment for high treason was on the books until 1870:

That you be drawn on a hurdle to the place of execution where you shall be hanged by the neck and being alive cut down, your privy members shall be cut off and your bowels taken out and burned before you, your head severed from your body and your body divided into four quarters to be disposed of at the King's pleasure.

In William Shakespeare's *Macbeth*, the old Thane of Cawdor was a traitor to King Duncan, but he died well. Malcom said to King Duncan:

[...] I have spoke
With one that saw him die: who did report
That very frankly he confess'd his treasons,
Implored your highness' pardon and set forth
A deep repentance: nothing in his life
Became him like the leaving it; he died
As one that had been studied in his death
To throw away the dearest thing he owed,
As 'twere a careless trifle.
(*Macbeth* 1.4.2-11, Signet Edition)

This is one kind of valor that Compass would encourage.

Sir Diaphanous Silkworm said, "But mine is a judicial resolving or liberal undertaking of a danger —"

The Fifth Kind of Valor: A nobleman shows valor when facing a risk worthy of a gentleman — such as a duel.

Compass interrupted, "— that might be avoided."

"Aye," Sir Diaphanous Silkworm said, "and with assurance that it is found in noblemen and gentlemen of the best sheaf — the best class."

Such risks are avoidable, and they are sometimes avoided.

Compass said, "Who having lives to lose, like ordinary private men, have yet a world of honor, and public reputation to defend —"

Sir Diaphanous Silkworm interrupted, "— which in the brave historified Greeks and Romans you shall read of."

They are historified — celebrated in history.

Compass said, "And, no doubt, many in our aldermen meet it, and their deputies, the soldiers of the city, valiant blades, who, rather than their houses should be ransacked, would fight it out like so many wild beasts, not for the fury they are commonly armed with, but the close manner of their fight and custom of joining head to head and foot to foot."

The alderman would fight to protect their property not by physically fighting but by presenting a unified front to the enemy.

Soldiers can fight in close formation: Roman armies were famous for doing that.

"And which of these so well-pressed and well-argued resolutions am I to encounter now?" Captain Ironside said. "For commonly men who have so much choice before them have some trouble to resolve and decide on any one of them."

Master Bias said, "There are three valors yet that Sir Diaphanous has, if he doesn't mind my saying so, not touched."

"Yeah?" Sir Diaphanous Silkworm said. "Which are those?"

Master Practice said quietly to Compass, "He perks up at that!"

Sir Diaphanous Silkworm had perked up because more discussion about valor meant putting off the duel for a while longer.

Compass said quietly to Master Practice, "Nay, he does more: He chatters."

Sir Diaphanous Silkworm's teeth could chatter out of fear.

Of course, more chatter from Master Bias meant putting off the duel.

Master Bias said:

"A philosophical contempt of death is one kind of valor."

Marcus Porcius Cato Uticensis — often called Cato the Younger — lived according to strict ethical principles. He fought against Julius Caesar, whom he believed wanted to do away with the Roman Republic and make himself King of Rome. After Julius Caesar defeated the army of Cato the Younger at Utica in Africa, Cato committed suicide after reading the *Phaedo*, a dialogue by Plato in which appear arguments for the immortality of the soul. Believing that his soul is immortal, Cato the Younger killed himself because he loved freedom and did not want to live in what he thought would become a kingdom rather than a republic.

The Sixth Kind of Valor: Fortitude that comes from philosophy.

"Then, an infused, instilled kind of valor wrought in us by our *genii* or good spirits and guardian angels, of which the gallant ethnics — heathens — had deep sense, who generally held that no great statesman, scholar, or soldier ever did anything *sine divino aliquo afflatu*."

The Latin quotation from Cicero's *De natura deorum*, or *On the Nature of the Gods*, 2.167, means "Without any divine inspiration."

The Seventh Kind of Valor: Fortitude that is a gift from non-Christian gods.

Master Practice said, "But there's a Christian valor above these, too."

Master Bias said, "Which is a quiet patient toleration of whatsoever the malicious world with injury does to you, and consists in passion more than action, Sir Diaphanous."

The passion of Christ is His suffering and death.

Some Christians believe that the virtue of patience and suffering display a greater valor than physical fortitude and courage.

The Eighth Kind of Valor: Christian patience and suffering.

Sir Diaphanous Silkworm said, "To be sure, I do take mine to be Christian valor —"

If he does, he need not fight but instead can suffer patiently.

"You may be mistaken, though," Compass said. "Can you justify on any reason this seeking to deface in a duel the divine image in a man?"

Exodus 20.13 states, "*Thou shalt not kill*" (King James Version).

Genesis 1:26 states, "*And God said, Let us make man in our image, after our likeness: and let them have dominion over the fish of the sea, and over the fowl of the air, and over the cattle, and over all the earth, and over every creeping thing that creepeth upon the earth*" (King James Version).

"Oh, sir!" Master Bias said. "Let them alone! Isn't Diaphanous as much a divine image as is Ironside? Let images fight, if they will fight, in God's name."

Both Sir Diaphanous Silkworm and Captain Ironside are divine images: images of God.

Master Bias would be happy if Captain Ironside were to kill Sir Diaphanous Silkworm.

Nurse Keep entered the scene and interrupted them.

"Where's Master Needle?" she asked. "Have you seen Master Needle? We are ruined!

"What ails the frantic, lunatic nurse?" Compass asked.

"My mistress is undone — she's crying out!" Nurse Keep said. "Where is this man, do you think? Where is Master Needle?"

Master Needle entered the scene and said, "Here I am."

"Run for the party whom we need: Mistress Chair, the midwife," Nurse Keep said.

Stupified by the request, Master Needle stood still.

Nurse Keep said, "Nay, look how the man stands, as if he were gowked — stupified! She's lost, if you do not hasten away from the party."

As would become clear, "she" is Placentia.

"Where is the doctor?" Master Needle asked.

Nurse Keep said:

"Where a scoffing, dismissive man is, and his apothecary is little better. They laugh and jeer at everything.

"Will you hurry?

"And fetch the person in question — the midwife — quickly to our mistress. We are all ruined! The tympany will out else!"

The tympany is a swelling. "The tympany will out" means 1) The baby will be born, and 2) The tympany — pregnancy — will become gossip.

Nurse Keep and Master Needle exited.

Sir Moth Interest entered the scene and said:

"News, news, good news, better than buttered news!"

Nathaniel Butter was an early newsman.

Sir Moth Interest continued:

"My niece is found with child, the doctor tells me, and has started labor."

"What!" Compass said.

"The portion's paid!" Sir Moth Interest said. "The portion —"

"The portion's paid!" means "the portion is a dead issue!" or "the portion is settled!"

In this society, a man of high position would not want to marry a woman who gave birth out of wedlock to another man's child. This meant that Sir Moth Interest would keep the dowry.

"Oh, the captain! Is he here?" Sir Moth Interest said, seeing Captain Ironside.

Sir Moth exited.

"He's spied your swords out," Master Practice said. "Put them away! Put them away! You've driven him away from here; and yet your quarrel's ended."

One quarrel was over who would get Placentia's dowry.

Captain Ironside said, "It has ended in a most strange discovery and revelation."

"Of light gold," Master Practice said.

"Light gold" is a gold coin that is no longer legal tender because its edges have been clipped to collect bits of gold. Gold coins had rings, aka circles, and if the clipping extended inside the circle, the coin was no longer legal tender.

Sir Diaphanous Silkworm said:

"And cracked within the ring."

One kind of circle or ring is a vagina. Placentia's vagina had been metaphorically "cracked," and in this society she was no longer regarded as wife material for an upper-class man.

Sir Diaphanous Silkworm said:

"I take the omen as a good omen."

The omen was birth. One way in which it was a good omen was that Sir Diaphanous Silkworm would not first marry Placentia and then discover that she was pregnant with another man's baby.

Master Practice said:

"Then put up — put away — your sword."

In the confusion, Compass exited.

Master Practice continued:

"And put on your doublet. Give the captain thanks."

The two would-be combatants sheathed their swords.

Putting on his doublet, Sir Diaphanous Silkworm said:

"I would have been slurred else."

He meant that his honor would have been stained due to being engaged to a woman who gave birth out of wedlock (assuming that he would have been chosen to be her husband).

He continued:

"Thank you, noble captain! Your quarrelling caused all this."

The quarreling had kept all of Placentia's suitors from being chosen to be engaged to and marry her.

"Where's Compass?" Captain Ironside asked.

Master Practice said, "Gone, shrunk hence, contracted to his center, I fear."

"Shrunk hence" can mean that Compass has shrunk away and left the scene.

A penis can shrink and contract, returning closer to a man's center.

Another kind of center could be the center of a target. A metaphorical target for Compass' "arrow" could be Placentia's vagina.

Master Practice suspected that Compass was the father of Placentia's child, and so Compass had gone to see her.

"The slip is his, then," Captain Ironside said.

Compass had given them the slip. A "slip" is also a counterfeit, illegitimate coin. A "slip" is also a sexual slip, and it is the baby that can result from a sexual slip.

Captain Ironside's words can be interpreted as saying that Compass was the father of Placentia's illegitimate baby.

Sir Diaphanous Silkworm said, "I was likely to have been abused in the business, had the slip slurred on me, a counterfeit."

The slip is the illegitimate child. Sir Diaphanous Silkworm could have married Placentia and been the non-biological father of a counterfeit — illegitimate and not his own — child.

Master Bias said, "Sir, we are all abused, as many as were brought on to be suitors, and we will all join in thanks to the captain, and to his fortune that so brought us off and rescued us."

Captain Ironside's coming unannounced to duel Sir Diaphanous Silkworm had helped both Sir Diaphanous and Master Bias by delaying the choice of a husband for Placentia. They could have been engaged to marry a woman who was now giving birth to another man's child.

Captain Ironside's fortune, aka luck, had also brought them good fortune.

— CHORUS 3 —

Damplay said, "This was a pitiful poor trick of your poet, boy, to make his prime woman character be with child — be pregnant — and fall into labor just to settle a quarrel."

John Trygust replied:

"With whose borrowed ears have you heard, sir, all this while, that you can mistake the current — the direction — of our scene so?

"The stream of the plot threatened her being with child from the very beginning, for it presented her in the first part of the second act with some apparent note of infirmity or defect, from knowledge of which the members of the audience were rightly to be left hanging and kept in suspense by the author until the quarrel, which was only the accidental, by-chance cause, hastened on the discovery of it in occasioning her fright, which made her fall into her throes of childbirth quickly, and all of this happened within that compass of time allowed to the comedy wherein the poet expressed his prime artifice — his primary artistic construction. It is not an error that the detection of her being with child should bring to an end the quarrel that had produced it."

"The boy is too hard for you, Brother Damplay," Probee said. "You had best pay attention to the play and let him alone."

"I don't care for marking — paying attention to — the play," Damplay said. "I'll damn it, talk, and do that which I have come for. I will not have gentlemen lose their privilege, nor I myself my prerogative, for never an overgrown or superannuated poet — fat and aged playwright — of them all! He shall not give me the law. I will censure and judge the play, and be witty, and take my tobacco, and enjoy my Magna Carta of reprehension and criticism, as my predecessors have done before me."

Damplay believed that since he is a gentleman, he has the right and prerogative to criticize the play.

The Magna Carta recognized upper-class people's right of free speech, including the right to criticize.

"Even to behavior and speech beyond control and absurdity," John Trygust said.

Probee said, "Not now, because the gentlewoman is in labor and the midwife may come on stage all the sooner, to put her and us out of our pain."

Damplay said to John Trygust, "Well, look to your business afterward, boy, that all things be clear and come properly forth, suited and set together in order; for I will search what follows severely and to the fingernail."

Sculptors would scrape a fingernail on a marble statue to check for flaws.

"Let your fingernail run smooth then and not scratch, lest the author be bold to pare your fingernail to the quick and make it hurt," John Trygust said. "You'll find him as severe as yourself."

Damplay said:

"He is a shrewd, cunning boy, and he has bested me everywhere!"

Seeing that the next scene was starting, he said:

"The midwife has come; she has made haste."

CHAPTER 4

— 4.1 —

Mother Chair and the midwife and Master Needle talked together.

"Stay, Master Needle, you do prick — hurry — too fast upon the business," Mother Chair said. "I must take some breath. Give me my stool. You have drawn a stitch — a sharp pain — in my side upon me, in faith, son Needle, with your haste.

A midwife would sit on the stool to assist at a childbirth. The pregnant woman would be in a birthing-chair, some of which were three-legged stools.

The words "mother" and "son" did not mean a biological relationship. They were simply words of etiquette.

Master Needle said, "Good mother, piece up — mend — this breach; I'll give you a new gown, a new silk grogram gown. I'll do it, mother."

A breach is a hole. Placentia's pregnancy was something that needed to be patched up. It was a bad situation, and Mother Chair and the midwife and Master Needle wanted to make it less bad.

"Grogram" is a coarse silk fabric.

Nurse Keep entered the room.

She had overheard Master Needle's last few words, and she said:

"What'll you do? You have done too much already with your prick-seam, and through-stitch, Master Needle."

A prick-seam is a kind of stitch used in making gloves, and a through-stitch is a stitch that is drawn through the material.

Hmm. The word "prick" has a bawdy meaning, and a needle can be likened to a male body part. Perhaps Compass is not the father of Placentia's baby. Perhaps there is an explanation for Master Needle's wanting to give Mother Chair a new silk grogram gown if she mends this breach.

Nurse Keep then said:

"I ask you to not sit fabling here old tales, good Mother Chair, the midwife. Just hurry and come up to Placentia's bed-chamber."

Mother Chair and Master Needle exited.

Compass and Master Practice entered the scene.

"How are things now, nurse? Where's My Lady?" Compass asked.

"My Lady" is Lady Loadstone.

"In her bed-chamber locked up, I think," Nurse Keep said. "She'll speak with nobody."

"Does she knows about this accident — this incident?" Compass asked.

"Alas, sir, no," Nurse Keep said. "I wish that she might never know about it!"

She exited.

Master Practice said, "I think Her Ladyship is too virtuous and too nobly innocent to have a hand in and take part in so ill-formed, badly conceived, and poorly managed a business."

The business was attempting to have Master Practice marry a woman who was pregnant with another man's baby.

Compass said:

"Your thought, sir, is a brave, admirable thought and a safe one. The child now to be born is not more free from the aspersion — soil and defamation — of all spot — stain and moral disgrace — than she.

"Even if there were no other considerations, would Lady Loadstone have her hand in a plot against Master Practice, whom she so loves, cries up and speaks well about, and values?"

Compass then mentioned the other reasons why Lady Loadstone would not be involved in a plot against Master Practice:

"Whom she knows to be a man marked out for a chief justice in his cradle? Or a lord paramount, the head of the Hall, aka master of an Inn of Court, the top or the top-gallant of our law?"

"Top" and "top-gallant" are high sails. Master Practice will rise high in his legal career.

Compass continued:

"Assure yourself, she could not so deprave and impair the rectitude of her judgment to wish you to a wife who might prove to bring infamy and bad reputation to you, a wife whom she esteemed that part of the commonwealth and had up for honor to her blood."

"I must confess a great beholdingness and obligation to Her Ladyship's offer and good wishes," Master Practice said. "But the truth is, I never had affection for or any liking of this niece of hers."

"You foresaw something, then?" Compass asked.

"I had my notes and my prognostics," Master Practice said.

"Notes" can mean gossip — people note what other people say and do.

"Prognostics" are foreknowledge: predictions of the future.

"You read almanacs and study them to some purpose, I believe?" Compass asked.

Almanacs were bound together with prognostics.

"I do confess it," Master Practice said. "I do believe and pray, too, according to the planets at some times."

According to astrology, some days are propitious for some tasks. Other days are not propitious for those tasks.

"And you do observe the sign of the zodiac in making love?" Compass asked.

In this society, "making love" meant wooing.

"As I do in phlebotomy," Master Practice said.

Phlebotomy is the medical procedure of opening a vein to let out blood. Some days were regarded as propitious for this procedure; these days were determined by astrology.

"And you choose your mistress — the woman whom you are devoted to — by the good days, and leave her by the bad?"

"I do, and I do not," Master Practice said.

In other words: I do choose her on the propitious days, and I do not choose her on the days that are not propitious.

Compass said to himself, "A little more would fetch all his astonomy from Allestree."

In other words: A little conversation would show that he got all his prognostications from a man named Allestree.

Astonomy is perhaps a portmanteau word meaning "astonishing astronomy." The phrase may be regarded as a description of astrology — which is the word that readers would expect to see there.

It would be astonishing if astrology were true.

Richard Allestree of Derby was a poor poet and an almanac writer. An enemy of Ben Jonson named Alexander Gill wrote that Allestree was a Homer in comparison to Jonson.

Master Practice said, "I tell you, Master Compass, as my friend, and under seal — in secret — I cast my eye long ago upon the other wench, My Lady's serving-woman. She is another manner of piece — a different kind of sexual object — for handsomeness than is the niece — but that is *sub sigillo* — under seal, a secret — as I give it you in hope of your aid and counsel in the business."

Compass said:

"You need counsel? You who are the only famous counsel of the kingdom and in all courts?"

"Counsel" can mean 1) advice, and 2) a lawyer.

Compass continued:

"That is a jeer, in faith, worthy your name and your profession, too, sharp Master Practice."

"Sharp" can mean 1) intelligent, and 2) cunning in an unethical sense. A "sharper" is a cheat — a swindler.

"Sharp practice" is unethical practice — unethical tricks.

Master Practice replied, "No, upon my law, as I am a bencher and now double reader, I meant in pure simplicity of request."

"Bencher" and "double reader" are positions in the Inns of Court, with "double reader" being the more senior position. The Inns of Court are buildings owned by legal associations.

Compass said:

"If you meant so."

He may have emphasized the "If."

He continued:

"The affairs are now perplexing and confused and full of trouble; give them time to breathe and to settle down.

"I'll do my best.

"But in the meantime, prepare the parson."

He said to himself:

"I am glad to know this, for I myself liked the young maiden before, and loved her, too."

Compass was happy because he could now use this information to keep Master Practice from marrying Pleasance.

Compass then asked out loud:

"Do you have you a marriage license?"

"No, but I can fetch one quickly," Master Practice said.

Compass said:

"Do, do, and remember the parson's pint to engage him in the business."

The parson's pint is a gift — or a bribe.

Compass added:

"A knitting cup there must be."

The knitting cup is a cup of wine that is passed around at weddings.

"I shall do it," Master Practice said.

He exited, leaving Compass behind.

Master Bias and Sir Moth Interest entered the scene.

Master Bias complained to Sir Moth Interest, "It is an affront to me from you, sir. You brought me here to My Lady's to woo a wife, who since has proved to be a cracked commodity. She is damaged merchandise. She has broken bulk too soon."

"Broken bulk" means "unloaded cargo." She gave birth too soon — she gave birth before being married.

Sir Moth Interest said:

"It is no fault of mine, if she is cracked in pieces or broke round."

"Broke round" means broken around the edges. Her value had been lessened the way the value of a coin is lessened when its circumference has been clipped.

One kind of "round" is a vagina, and her virginity had been broken the way a hymen can be broken.

Sir Moth Interest continued:

"It was the fault of my sister, who owns the house where my niece has got her clap, which makes all this uproar."

The clap can mean 1) misfortune, 2) venereal disease, and/or 3) loud noise.

Sir Moth Interest continued:

"I keep her marriage portion safe; that is not scattered.

"The moneys don't rattle, nor are they thrown to make a muss yet among the gamesome — merry — suitors."

According to the *Oxford English Dictionary*, the verb "rattle" can mean "to give out a rapid succession of short, sharp, percussive sounds."

Also according to the *Oxford English Dictionary*, the noun "rattle" can mean "A state of uproar, commotion, or boisterous or exuberant activity" (first entry 1688; *The Magnetic Lady* was licensed for performance on 12 October 1632).

A rapid succession of short, sharp, percussive sounds uttered during exuberant activity could be this: "Oh! Oh! Oh! Oh! Oh!"

"Muss" is a scrambling and snatching game.

Compass said:

"Can you endure that flouting insult, close — secretive — Master Bias, who have been so bred in the politics?

"The injury is done to you, and by him only. He lent you impressed money, and he upbraids you with it."

"Impressed money" is money that is paid in advance. Sir Moth Interest had given Master Bias 400 pounds so that he could buy new clothes and make a good impression on Lady Loadstone and Placentia. This money was an advance on the dowry that Master Bias would get if he married Placentia.

Compass continued:

"He has furnished you with money for the wooing, and now waives — disregards — you. He casts you aside."

"That makes me expostulate — complain about — the wrong so with him, and that makes me resent it as I do," Master Bias said.

"But do it home, then," Compass said. "Carry this matter — this complaint — to a conclusion."

"Sir, my lord shall know it," Master Bias said.

"And all the lords of the court, too," Compass said.

"What a moth you are, Sir Interest!" Master Bias said.

"In what way am I a moth, I ask you, Sweet Master Bias?" Sir Moth Interest asked.

Compass answered, "To draw in young statesmen and heirs of policy into the noose of an infamous matrimony."

The verb "to moth" meant "to hunt for moths." Sir Moth Interest hunted for moths such as Master Bias who, like Sir Moth Interest, were drawn to Placentia's marriage portion the way that a moth is drawn to a candle.

"Heirs of policy" are those who are likely to gain political power.

Master Bias said:

"Yes, infamous and shameful, *quasi in communem famam.*"

The Latin *quasi in communem famam* means "as though in a public scandal."

A marriage to Placentia would be a public scandal.

Master Bias continued:

"And matrimony, *quasi* [as if] matter of money."

This means "marriage as if it were for the sake of money."

Indeed, Placentia's suitors were after her marriage portion.

"Learnedly urged, my cunning Master Bias," Compass said.

Master Bias said, "Matrimony — matter of money — with his lewd, known, and prostituted niece."

Master Bias meant that Sir Moth Interest wanted him to marry Placentia although she were known to be lewd.

A marriage to Placentia would be a public scandal.

"Lewd" can mean 1) unchaste, 2) uneducated, and 3) evil.

Sir Moth Interest said:

"My known and prostitute!"

As an adjective, the word "prostitute" means "licentitious."

Sir Moth Interest continued:

"How you mistake the situation and run upon a false ground, Master Bias!

"Your political lords will do me right."

Sir Moth Interest meant that he did not know that Placentia was a lewd woman until now.

Also, if there were to be a trial about Placentia's dowry, which he wanted to keep, he hoped that the lords of the Inns of Court would support him.

Sir Moth Interest continued:

"Now she is prostitute and now that I know it — please understand me — I mean to keep the marriage portion in my hands and pay no moneys."

Compass said:

"Did you mark that, Don Bias? Are you paying attention?"

"Don" is a complimentary title, but Compass meant that Master Bias had been "done": manipulated and taken advantage of.

Compass continued:

"And you shall still remain in bonds to Sir Moth for wooing furniture and impressed charges."

Master Bias had been furnished with money in advance to buy furniture — clothing and gifts — so he could woo Placentia in style and impress her.

"Good Master Compass, for the sums Master Bias has had from me, I do acquit him," Sir Moth Interest said. "They are his own. Here before you I do release him."

"Good!" Compass said.

"Oh, sir!" Master Bias said.

Compass said to Master Bias, "By God's eyelid, take it. I do witness it. Sir Moth cannot hurl away his money better."

Sir Moth Interest said, "Master Bias shall get so much, sir, by my acquaintance, to be my friend. And now report to his lords as I deserve no otherwise."

Master Bias would not have to repay the 400 pounds he had gotten from Sir Moth Interest. In return, he would be Sir Moth Interest's friend at court.

Compass said:

"You deserve no otherwise but well, and I will witness it and I will be witness to the value: Four hundred pounds is the price, if I am not mistaken, of your true friend in court.

"Shake hands. You have bought him, and you have bought him cheap."

Sir Moth Interest and Master Bias shook hands.

"I am His Worship's servant," Master Bias said.

Master Bias had been bribed and would now be Sir Moth Interest's advocate at court.

Compass said to himself, "And you are his slave, Sir Moth. Sealed and delivered. Haven't you studied the court compliment?"

The "court compliment" is a court ceremony. In this case, it is the ceremony of buying a courtier.

Sir Moth Interest and Master Bias exited.

Compass said to himself, "Here are a pair of humors reconciled now, whom money held at a distance and kept them apart from each other; or their thoughts, which are baser than money."

Their base thoughts are love of money.

Money is not the root of all evil — love of money is.

Both men wanted Placentia's dowry. Both men would have gotten a portion of it if Master Bias had married her. But Master Bias had been angry at Sir Moth Interest because Placentia was pregnant. He was also angry at having to repay the 400 pounds that he had been given in advance to woo Placentia.

The argument had been resolved by Master Bias becoming Sir Moth Interest's friend at court in return for not having to repay the 400 pounds.

Ben Jonson's play is subtitled "humors reconciled," and these are the first two humors to be reconciled.

Mistress Polish and Nurse Keep entered the scene. They were arguing, quietly at first and then louder. They did not see Compass.

Mistress Polish said to Nurse Keep, "Get out, thou caitiff — base — witch! Bawd, beggar, gypsy! Anything indeed but an honest woman!"

"Whatever you please, Dame Polish, My Lady's stroker and flatterer," Nurse Keep said.

Compass said to himself, "What is going on here? The gossips have fallen out with each other!"

Madame Polish said to Nurse Keep, "Thou are a traitor to me, an Eve, the apple, and the serpent, too. Thou are a viper that has eaten a passage through me, through my own bowels, by thy recklessness."

Vipers were thought to be born by biting their way out of their mother's body. They were symbols of ingratitude.

Compass said to himself, "What frantic outburst is this? I'll step aside and listen to it."

He hid himself.

Madame Polish said:

"Did I trust thee, wretch, with such a secret of that consequence, which did so concern me and my child, our livelihood and reputation? And have thou undone and ruined us? By thy connivance with an evil person, with you nodding and napping in a corner, and allowing her to be gotten with child so basely?

"Sleepy, unlucky hag! Thou bird of night and all mischance to me!"

Birds of night are birds of ill omen.

"Good lady empress!" Nurse Keep said. "Had I the keeping of your daughter's clicket — latch — in charge? Was that committed to my trust?"

A clicket is the latch of a door or a gate. "Clicket" is also a word metaphorically related to sex. Think of a key being inserted into a lock. A latch-key raises the latch of a door or a gate. Doors and gates can be open or closed.

Compass said, "Her daughter?"

Mistress Polish's daughter was Pleasance. Was Pleasance pregnant, like Placentia?

Compass wanted to marry Pleasance.

Mistress Polish said, "Softly, devil, not so loud. You'd have the house hear and be witness, would you?"

"Let all the world be witness," Nurse Keep said. "Before I'll endure the tyranny of such a tongue — and of such a pride —"

"What will you do?" Mistress Polish asked.

Nurse Keep answered:

"Tell truth and shame the she-man-devil in puffed sleeves!"

A proverb stated, "Tell truth and shame the devil."

The "she-man-devil" wearing puffed sleeves is Mistress Polish.

Nurse Keep continued:

"Run any hazard by revealing all to My Lady about how you changed the cradles and changed the children in them!"

"Not so high!" Mistress Polish said. "Not so loud!"

Nurse Keep's voice traveled.

Nurse Keep said, "Calling your daughter Pleasance there 'Placentia,' and calling my true mistress Placentia by the name of 'Pleasance.'"

Not only had the babies been exchanged, but their names had also been exchanged.

To avoid confusion, this book will continue to use the name "Placentia" for the woman who has hitherto been called Placentia, and this book will continue to use the name "Pleasance" for the woman who has hitherto been called Pleasance.

Compass said to himself, "A horrid and detestable secret, this is — and it's worth the discovery!"

Pleasance was actually Lady Loadstone's niece, while Placentia was actually Mistress Polish's daughter.

Suitors had been trying to marry Placentia for the dowry, but the dowry actually belonged to Pleasance.

In Homer's *Odyssey* the suitors were trying to marry Penelope and become the King of Ithaca, but Penelope's husband, Odysseus, was still alive. His palace still belonged to him.

"And must you be thus loud?" Mistress Polish asked.

Nurse Keep said:

"I will be louder, and I will cry it through the house, through every room, and every office — workplace — of the laundry-maids, until it is borne hot to My Lady's ears.

"Before I will live in such a slavery, I'll do away myself. I'll kill myself."

"Didn't thou swear to keep it secret?" Mistress Polish said. "And upon what book? I remember now: *The Practice of Piety*."

Lewes Bayly, Bishop of Bangor, wrote *The Practice of Piety*, which was a Puritan devotional manual.

Nurse Keep said:

"It was a practice of impiety out of your wicked forge and making. I know it now — my conscience tells me."

Forges work with metal, and Mistress Polish had worked evil on the Steel family. Lady Loadstone was the widow of a man named Steel.

Nurse Keep continued:

"First, it was a practice of impiety against the infants, to rob them of their names and their true parents.

"Second, it was a practice of impiety to abuse the neighborhood, to keep them in error.

"Third, and most of all, it was a practice of impiety against My Lady. She has the main wrong, and I will let her know it instantly.

"Repentance, if it is true, never comes too late."

Midwives, nurses, and guardians had the ethical duty not to switch babies. Parents wanted to raise their own children and leave the inheritance to them, not to other children.

Switching children would also abuse the neighborhood. If a midwife, nurse, or guardian switched one child, perhaps she had switched or would switch other children.

Nurse Keep exited.

Mistress Polish said:

"What have I done? Conjured a spirit up I shall not lay down again? Drawn a danger and ruin on myself thus, by provoking a peevish fool whom nothing will persuade to stop or will satisfy, I fear?

"Her patience stirred has turned to fury.

"I have run my bark — my ship — on a 'sweet' rock by my own arts and trust, and I must get off again, or be dashed to pieces!"

She exited.

"This was a business worth the listening after," Compass said to himself.

— 4.5 —

Pleasance, the true niece of Lady Loadstone, entered the scene and said:

"Oh, Master Compass, did you see my mother?

"Mistress Placentia, My Lady's niece, was newly brought to bed of the bravest — most splendid — boy!

"Will you go see it?"

"First, I'll know the father, before I approach these hazards," Compass replied.

He did not want to cause gossip that he was the faather.

Pleasance said, "Mistress Midwife has promised to find out a father for it, if there is need."

The father need not be the biological father.

"She may the safelier — the more safely — do it by virtue of her place as a midwife," Compass said. "But, pretty Pleasance, I have a piece of news for you that I think will please you."

"What is it, Master Compass?" Pleasance asked.

"Wait, you must earn it before you know it," Compass said. "Where's My Lady?"

"She has retired to her chamber and shut it up," Pleasance said.

"She has heard nothing about this yet?" Compass said. "Well, command the coach to be made ready and prepare yourself to travel a little way with me."

"To where, for God's sake?" Pleasance asked.

"Where I'll entreat you to do something not to your loss, believe it, if you dare trust yourself," Compass said.

"I will go with you the world over!" Pleasance said.

"The news will well requite the pains, I assure you, and in this tumult you will not be missed," Compass said. "Command the coach to be made ready. It is an instant — an urgent — business that will not be done without you."

Pleasance exited, and Parson Palate entered the scene.

Compass said, "Parson Palate, we are most opportunely met. Step into my chambers. I'll come to you soon. There is a friend or two who will entertain and receive you."

Parson Palate exited, and Master Practice, who was holding a marriage license, entered the scene.

Compass asked, "Master Practice, do you have the license?"

"Here it is," Master Practice said.

"Let's see it," Compass said. "Your name's not in it."

"I'll fill that in soon," Master Practice said. "It has the seal, which is the main thing, and it is registered. The clerk knows me and trusts me."

"Do you have the parson?" Compass asked.

"They say he's here," Master Practice said. "He said that he would come here."

Compass said:

"I would not have him seen here for a world, to breed suspicion. Intercept him and prevent that. But take your license with you and fill in the blank, or leave it here with me. I'll do it for you."

Compass would both intercept the parson and fill in the blank. Actually, he had already intercepted the parson.

Compass continued:

"Wait for us at his church behind the Old Exchange; we'll come in the coach and meet you there within this quarter of an hour at least."

Master Practice gave him the marriage license and said:

"I am much bound to you, Master Compass. You have all the law and parts — abilities — of Squire Practice forever at your use.

"I'll tell you news, too. Sir, your reversion's fallen. Thinwit, Surveyor of the Projects General, is dead."

This meant that Compass would become the new Surveyor of the Projects General. This was a desirable position.

"When did he die?" Compass asked.

"Just this morning," Master Practice said. "I received the news from a right hand: an important aide."

"Conceal it, Master Practice, and bear in mind the main affair you have in hand and are actively concerned with," Compass said.

Master Practice exited the scene, and Pleasance entered the scene.

"The coach is ready, sir," Pleasance said.

Compass said:

"It is well, fair Pleasance, although now we shall not use it."

He had intended for the coach to take Pleasance and him to the church to be married. Now the coach was not needed. Parson Palate and a marriage license were here.

Compass continued:

"Tell the coachman to drive to the parish church and stay about there until Master Practice comes to him and employs him."

Pleasance exited.

Compass said to himself, "I have a license now that must be registered before my lawyer's license."

"My lawyer" is Master Practice.

Master Practice was not his lawyer. Compass was using "my" the same way a person might say "my boy," when referring to a boy who was not his son.

Parson Palate entered the scene.

Compass said to him, "Noble Parson Palate, thou shall be a mark advanced: Here's a piece. And do a feat — an action — for me."

Nobles, marks, and pieces are coins.

"What, Master Compass?" Parson Palate asked.

Compass answered, "Just run — speak — the words of matrimony over my head and Mistress Pleasance's in my chamber. There's Captain Ironside to be a witness, and here's a license to make thee feel secure that the wedding is legitimate, Parson!"

Parson Palate did not look happy.

Compass asked, "What do you stick at? Why are you hesitating?"

Parson Palate said:

"It is afternoon, sir, directly against the canon law — the ecclesiastical law — of the church."

According to the ecclesiastical law of the time and place, weddings had to take place between the hours of eight and twelve in the morning. Also, the wedding had to take place at a church.

Parson Palate continued:

"You know it, Master Compass, and besides, I am hired by and committed to our worshipful friend, the learnèd Master Practice, in that business."

He was supposed to officiate at the marriage of Master Practice and Pleasance.

Compass said:

"Come on, engage yourself — commit yourself. Who shall be able to say you married us other than in the morning, the most canonical and legal minute of the day, if you affirm it?"

Compass wanted Parson Palate to lie about the time of the wedding and to break his previous commitment and promise made to Master Practice.

He continued:

"That's a spiced — over-scrupulous — excuse, and it shows you have set the common law before any profession — religious vow — else of love or friendship."

According to Compass' rhetoric, Parson Palate was preferring the interests of Master Practice the lawyer over his religious vow to prefer the interests of love and friendship.

Pleasance had agreed to go with Compass the world over — that was evidence of love and friendship — and their marriage would also be evidence of love and friendship.

There is no evidence that Master Practice had even asked Pleasance to marry him, much less that she had accepted his proposal.

Pleasance returned.

Compass said to her, "Come, Mistress Pleasance, we cannot prevail with the rigid parson here."

He then said to Parson Palate, "But, sir, I'll keep you locked in my lodging until it is done elsewhere, and under fear of Ironside."

Captain Ironside would guard him — a terrifying prospect to Parson Palate. While he was under guard, Parson Palate could not tell Master Practice what was happening.

"Do you hear me, sir?" Parson Palate said. "Listen to me."

"No, no, it doesn't matter," Compass said.

Parson Palate said:

"Can you think, sir, that I would deny you anything? I would not even if it meant the loss of both my livings. I will do it for you."

A living is a source of income; for example, a position as a vicar or other church official. Many parsons had more than one living.

Parson Palate asked:

"Do you have a wedding ring?"

Compass answered, "Aye, and a posy: *Annulus hic nobis quod scit uterque dabit.*"

A posy is a sentiment inscribed on the inside of a ring.

"Good!" Parson Palate said.

He loosely translated the posy: "This ring will give you what you both desire."

He then said, "I'll make the whole house chant it, and the parish."

Literally, the Latin states: "This ring will give to us what each knows."

Pleasance has yet to know that she is the daughter of Lady Loadstone; this is knowledge that Compass will give her. Readers will soon see that Pleasance has important knowledge to give to Compass.

"Why, well said, parson," Compass said.

He then said, "Now I will give to you my news that comprehends my reasons for this action, Mistress Pleasance."

Mother Chair, Master Needle, Mistress Polish, and Nurse Keep spoke together.

"Go, get a nurse, procure her at what rate you can, and out of the house with it, son Needle," Mother Chair said. "It is a bad commodity — a bad piece of goods."

"It" is the baby, which needed a wet nurse to breastfeed it.

"Good mother, I know it, but the best should now be made of it," Master Needle said.

They needed to make the best of a bad situation, and they needed to do what they could for the baby.

Mother Chair replied:

"And it shall."

Master Needle exited.

Mother Chair then said:

"You should not fret so, Mistress Polish, nor you, Dame Keep. My daughter shall do well, when she has taken my caudle — my medicinal drink. I have known twenty such breaches of trust pieced up and patched up and made whole without a bum of noise."

Placentia was not Mother Chair's biological daughter; "my daughter" was a term of etiquette.

Mother Chair meant "without a hum of noise," but "bum" goes well with "breeches." A bum of noise is a bum of farts.

A breach of trust can also be a vagina that has been breached out of wedlock. Mother Chair has known twenty out-of-wedlock births that ended well.

Of course, another breach of trust was the switching of babies.

Yet another breach of trust was the falling out between Mistress Polish and Nurse Keep.

"You two fall out?" Mother Chair said. "And you tear up one another?"

"Blessèd woman!" Mistress Polish said. "Blest be the peacemaker."

Nurse Keep said:

"The pease-dresser!"

A "pease-dresser" is someone who prepares peas for cooking.

The word "'pease" means "appease."

Nurse Keep continued:

"I'll hear no peace from Mistress Polish. I have been wronged. So has My Lady, My good Lady's Worship, and I will right her, hoping she'll right me."

Mistress Polish said, "Good gentle Keep, I ask thee, Mistress Nurse, to pardon my passion, to pardon my strong emotion. I was misadvised — I acted unadvisedly. Be thou yet better by this grave sage woman, Mother Chair, who is the mother of matrons and great persons and knows the world."

Nurse Keep said, "I do confess, she knows something — and I know something —"

She knew something Mistress Polish did not want Lady Loadstone to learn.

"Put your somethings together then," Mistress Polish said.

Mother Chair said:

"Aye, here's a chance fallen out that you cannot help, and less can this gentlewoman help.

"I can and will for both.

"First, I have sent by-chop away; the cause gone, the fame ceases."

In other words: Remove the cause of the gossip, and the gossip ceases.

The "by-chop" is the bastard. It is a by-blow: 1) a man's illegitimate child, and 2) a side-blow not directed at the main target. The man's "arrow" was not aimed at and did not hit the main target: a wife's vagina.

Mother Moth said:

"Then, by my caudle [medicinal drink] and my cullis [meat broth], I set my daughter on her feet about the house here. She's young and must stir and arouse herself somewhat for necessity. Her youth will bear it out: She's young enough to do it.

"She shall pretend to have had hysteria — a fit of the mother — and that is all that is needed if you have but a secretary laundress — one who can keep secrets — to blanch and whiten the linen."

Placentia would get up and be active and pretend that she had not given birth: "Baby? What baby?"

A laundress who could keep a secret would wash the bloodstained sheets.

"Take the former counsels — confidences — into you; keep them safe in your own breasts, and make your market of them at the highest."

The best market and the best price for the secrets involved keeping them secret. They still hoped to get a good marriage for Placentia. Such a marriage could benefit them as well as benefit Placentia.

Mother Chair continued:

"Will you go peach — turn informer — and proclaim yourself to be a fool at Grannam's Cross?"

Grannam's Cross was a public place. "Grannam" means "Old Woman," and "cross" is a crossroad.

Mother Chair continued:

"Will you be laughed at and despised?

"Will you betray a purpose that the deputy of a double ward or even his alderman with twelve of the wisest questmen — officials who investigate misdemeanors — could find out? Will you betray a purpose to these officials who are employed by the authority of the city?"

The purpose of switching babies was to secure a high social position for Mistress Polish's daughter. Punishment for such an action would be heavy.

Mother Chair continued:

"Come, come, be friends, and keep these women-matters, smock-secrets, women's secrets, to ourselves in our own verge, aka jurisdiction.

"We shall mar all if once we open the mysteries of the attiring house — dressing rooms — and tell what's done within.

"No theaters are more cheated with — tricked by — appearances, or these shop-lights, than the age is, and folk in them, who seem most curious — most careful."

Theaters rely on deception, and seeing things as they really are can be disappointing. The dashing young figure on stage may be a tired middle-aged man off stage.

Shop-lights can be kept low so that customers cannot closely inspect the merchandise on sale.

Our age, and we people in our age, are very badly tricked by appearances. Think of United States Supreme Court Justices who gave the appearance at their confirmation hearings that they believed that *Roe v. Wade* was settled law. Think of United States Senators who pretended to be shocked that those United States Supreme Court Justices had lied at their confirmation hearings.

Mistress Polish said:

"Breath of an oracle! You shall be my dear mother, wisest woman who ever tipped her tongue with point of reasons to turn — persuade — her hearers! She has sharpened her tongue with persuasive points as sharp as arrow tips. Mistress Keep, relent!"

She knelt and continued:

"I did abuse thee, I confess as far as to do penance, and on my knees I ask thee for forgiveness."

Mother Chair said, "Rise. She does begin to melt, I see it —"

"Nothing grieved me as much as when you called me 'bawd,'" Nurse Keep said. "'Witch' did not trouble me, nor 'gypsy,' no, nor 'beggar.' But 'bawd' was such a terrible name!"

Mother Chair said:

"No more rehearsals. No more repeating old words."

Mistress Polish rose.

Mother Chair continued:

"Repetitions make things worse. The more we stir — you know the proverb, and it signifies a — stink."

A proverb stated, "The more you stir, the more you stink."

Mother Chair continued:

"What's done and dead, let it be buried. New hours will fit fresh handles to new thoughts."

In other words: Time will heal their differences.

They exited.

Sir Moth Interest stood in a room with his footboy.

He ordered the footboy, "Run to the church, sirrah. Get all the drunkards to ring the bells and jangle them for joy. My niece has brought an heir to the house, a lusty — a vigorous and lively — boy."

The footboy exited.

Sir Moth Interest then asked himself, "Where's my sister Loadstone?"

Lady Loadstone entered the room.

Sir Moth Interest said to her:

"Asleep during afternoons! It is not wholesome, against all rules of health, lady sister. The little doctor will not like it.

"Our niece is newly delivered of a chopping — vigorous — child, who can call the father by his name already, if it just opens its mouth round."

Like other people, Sir Moth Interest thought that Compass was the father. The instrument with two legs and a movable joint that is used to make circles is known as a compass, and the baby would be saying "Compass" if it opened its mouth wide.

Hmm. "Instrument with two legs and a movable joint that is used to make circles." Yep, that's bawdy.

Sir Moth Interest continued:

"Master Compass, he is the man, they say, rumor gives it out, who has done that act of 'honor' to our house and friendship, to pump out a son and heir who shall inherit nothing, surely nothing, from me at least."

Illegitimate children who are known to be illegitimate often inherit little or nothing.

Compass entered the room.

Sir Moth Interest continued:

"I come to invite Your Ladyship to be a witness — a godmother."

Puritans did not use the word "godparent," but instead used the word "witness." Mistress Polish was a Puritan, and so was Lady Loadstone's and Sir Moth Interest's dead sister.

Sir Moth Interest continued:

"I will be your partner and give it a horn spoon and a treen dish — the badges of bastards and beggars — with a blanket for dame the doxy — Madam Slut — to march round the circuit with bag and baggage — with all her possessions."

A horn spoon was an inexpensive spoon made out of horn. A christening-gift for an upper-class infant was usually two silver spoons, each decorated with the image of an apostle.

A treen dish is a wooden bowl. Beggars used bowls in their begging.

Prostitutes walked behind a cart as they were paraded in public and mocked as punishment.

Compass said:

"Thou malicious knight, envious Sir Moth, who eats on that which feeds thee and frets — gnaws — her goodness who sustains thy being!"

Sir Moth Interest was biting the hand that fed him. That hand belonged to Lady Loadstone.

A proverb states, "Envy eats nothing but her own heart."

Compass continued:

"What company of mankind would acknowledge thy brotherhood, except as thou have a title — a claim — to her blood whom thy ill-nature has chosen to insult and triumph over and she be thus vexed over an accident in her house as if it were her crime, good innocent lady!

"Sir Moth Interest, thou show thyself to be a true corroding vermin, such as thou art."

Corroding vermin eat into their prey. The word "corrody" means a right to free quarters given by a lord or a religious house.

"Why, gentle Master Compass?" Sir Moth Interest said. "Because I wish you joy of your young son and heir to the house whom you have sent us?"

Sarcastically, Compass replied:

"Whom I have sent you? I don't know what I shall do."

Actually, he knew what he would do: He would call into the room some witnesses:

"Come in, friends."

Captain Ironside, Sir Diaphanous Silkworm, Master Bias, and Pleasance entered the room.

Compass said to Lady Loadstone, "Madam, I ask you to be pleased to trust yourself to our company."

Lady Loadstone replied:

"I did that too recently, and it brought this calamity upon me with all the infamy I hear.

"Your soldier, that swaggering, quarrelsome guest —"

Compass interrupted:

"— who has returned here to you as our vowed friend and servant, comes to sup with you — and so we do all — and who will prove he has deserved that special respect and favor from you.

"Your fortunes with yourself to boot — in addition — cast on a featherbed and spread on the sheets under a brace — a pair — of your best Persian carpets, would scarcely be a price valuable enough to thank his happy merit."

"Persian carpets" are bed and table coverings.

According to Compass, Captain Ironside had done something for Lady Loadstone that deserved to be repaid with all Lady Loadstone's fortune and with Lady Loadstone herself.

"What impudence is this?" Sir Moth Interest asked. "Can you endure to hear it, sister?"

Compass said:

"Yes, and you shall hear it, who will endure it worse."

Sir Moth Interest will suffer from hearing the news more than Lady Loadstone will.

Compass continued:

"What does he deserve in your opinion, madam, or your weighed judgment, he who — things thus hanging as they do in doubt, suspended and suspected, all involved and wrapped in error — can resolve the knot; redintegrate — restore and make perfect again — the reputation, first, of your house; restore Your Ladyship's quiet; render and restore then your niece a virgin who is unvitiated and unspoiled; and make all plain and perfect, as it was?

"What deserves the man who can stop a practice — a trick — to betray you and your name, and who can make all things right again?"

"He speaks impossibilities," Sir Moth Interest said.

Compass drew Captain Ironside forward, and then he said:

"Here he stands whose fortune has done this, and you must thank him. To what you call his swaggering and quarrelsomeness, we owe all this.

"And that it may have credit with you, madam, here is your niece, whom I have married. These gentlemen — the knight, captain, and parson, and this grave and serious politic tell-truth of the court — witnessed the wedding."

The "politic tell-truth" was Master Bias, who told the truth when it was politic to do so.

These people were able to confirm that Compass and Pleasance were married.

"Who is she whom I call niece, then?" Lady Compass asked.

If Pleasance were her niece, then who was Placentia?

Compass answered:

"She is Polish's daughter. Her mother, Goody Polish, has confessed to Grannam Keep, the nurse, how they exchanged the children in their cradles."

Lower-class women were called "Goody" or "Goodwife" as a respectful title.

"Grannam" meant 1) grandmother, or 2) old woman.

"For what purpose?" Lady Loadstone asked.

Compass answered, "To get the marriage portion, or some part of it."

He then said to Sir Moth Interest, "You must now disburse the entire marriage portion to me, sir, providing that I gain Her Ladyship's consent."

"I bid God give you joy, if what you say is true," Lady Loadstone said.

Compass said to her, "As true it is, lady, lady, in the song with the refrain 'lady, lady.'"

One song that includes the words "lady, lady" is "There dwelt a man in Babylon," about a woman named "Susannah," who was true and loyal to her husband, Joacim.

"Susanna," the source of and inspiration for the song, is an apocryphal book that is sometimes printed in Bibles.

Compass then said:

"The marriage portion's mine with interest, Sir Moth.

"I will not 'bate you a single harington of interest upon interest. I won't give you a single farthing.

"In the meantime, I commit you to the guard of Captain Ironside, my brother here, Captain Rudhudibras, from whom I will expect you or your ransom."

The ransom would pay for Sir Moth Interest's release from Captain Ironside.

"Sir, you must prove it and the possibility, before I believe it," Sir Moth Interest said.

Compass would have to provide evidence that what he claimed was true. He would have to explain what had happened and how it had happened.

Compass replied:

"For the possibility, I leave to trial.

"Truth shall speak itself."

Master Practice entered the scene.

"Oh, Master Practice, did you meet the coach?" Compass asked him.

"Yes, sir, but it was empty," Master Practice said.

Compass said:

"Why, I sent it for you. The business was dispatched here before you came.

"Come in, I'll tell you how. You are a man who will look for satisfaction and must have it."

The satisfaction could be sought in a duel, or in a court of law. The latter was more likely.

All said, "So do we all, and long to hear the right — the truth that will make everything all right."

— CHORUS 4 —

Damplay said, "Truly, I am one of those who labor with the same longing for the right, for it is almost puckered and tangled and pulled into that knot by your poet, which I cannot easily, with all the strength of my imagination, untie."

John Trygust replied, "Likely enough, nor is it in your office to be troubled or perplexed and confused with it, but to sit still and wait. The more your imagination busies itself, the more it becomes entangled, especially if (as I said in the beginning) you happen to find the wrong end."

Probee said:

"He has answered sufficiently well, Brother Damplay.

"Our roles, which are the spectators who would hear a comedy, are to await the process and progress and outcome of things, as the poet presents them, not as we would corruptly fashion them.

"We come here to see plays and censure — judge — them as they are made and fitted and prepared for us, not to beslaver our own thoughts with censorious spittle tempering the poet's clay as if we were to mold every scene anew. That would be a mere plastic ambition — creator's invention — or potter's ambition, most unbecoming the name of a gentleman."

In other words: Audiences should allow the playwright to do his work without interference.

Probee continued:

"Let us pay attention and not lose the business on foot — in progress — by talking. Let us follow the right thread or find it."

Damplay said, "Why, here his play might have ended, if he would have let it, and have spared us the vexation of a fifth act yet to come, which everyone here knows the issue of already, or may in part conjecture."

Many comedies end with a marriage, but this play still has a few loose ends: Who is the father of Placentia's baby? Will Sir Moth Interest hand over the marriage portion?

John Trygust said, "That conjecture is a kind of figure-flinging and astrological forecasting, or throwing the dice, for a meaning that was never in the poet's purpose, perhaps. Stay and see his last act, his *catastrophe* — the outcome and final turn of events. See how he will perplex that, or spring some fresh cheat or surprise, to entertain the spectators with a convenient and appropriate delight, until some unexpected and new encounter breaks out to rectify all and make good the conclusion."

In other words: We don't have a happy ending yet. Ben Jonson still has a few plot elements to surprise the audience.

Probee said, "The play, ending here, would have shown itself to be dull, flat, and unpointed, without a clear purpose, without any shape or sharpness, Brother Damplay."

"Well, let us wait and expect more then," Damplay said. "And may the poet's wit and intelligence help us."

CHAPTER 5

— 5.1 —

Master Needle and Tim Item talked together.

Master Needle said, "In truth, Master Item, here's a house divided and quartered into parts by your doctor's engine — his ingenious invention: He's cast out such aspersions and false insinuations on My Lady's niece here, of having had a child, as hardly will be wiped off, I doubt."

"Why, isn't it true?" Tim Item asked.

"True!" Master Needle said. "Did you think it to be true?"

"Wasn't she in labor?" Tim Item asked. "Wasn't the midwife sent for?"

"There's your error now!" Master Needle said. "You have drunk of the same water. You believe what they believe!

"I believed it, and I gave it out as the truth, too," Tim Item said. "I told it to others because I believed it."

"More you wronged the party," Master Needle said. "She had no such thing about her, innocent creature!"

"What had she then?" Tim Item asked.

"Only a fit of the mother!" Master Needle said. "She had a fit of hysteria! They burnt old shoes, goose-feathers, *asafoetida*, a few horn shavings, with a bone or two, and she is well again, and about the house —"

Asafoetida was a gum that was used as an antispasmodic.

"— is it possible?" Tim Item interrupted.

"See it, and then report it," Master Needle replied.

"Our doctor's urinal-judgment is half cracked, then," Tim Item said.

Doctors examined a patient's urine when diagnosing illness.

A half-cracked judgment is a judgment based on stupidity and ignorance.

"Cracked in the case most hugely, with My Lady and sad Sir Moth, her brother, who is now under a cloud a little," Master Needle said.

A "case" can be a vagina.

"Of what?" Tim Item asked. "Disgrace?"

"He is committed into the custody of Rudhudibras, the Captain Ironside, because of displeasure from Master Compass, but it will blow off," Master Needle said.

"The doctor shall reverse this instantly and set all right again, if you'll assist in just a toy, a trifling matter, Squire Needle, that comes in my noddle — my head — now," Tim Item said.

"Good — Needle and Noddle!" Master Needle said. "What may it be? I long for it."

Tim Item said, "Why, just to go to bed and feign a distemper — a disorder — of walking in your sleep and talking in it a little idly and without sense, but so much as on it the doctor may have the grounds to raise a cure for his reputation."

By "curing the illness," Doctor Rut would "cure" his damaged reputation. Some people now knew him as the doctor who did not diagnose Placentia's pregnancy.

"Anything to serve the worship — good name — of the man I love and honor," Master Needle said.

Mistress Polish and Pleasance met each other.

Pleasance still believed that Mistress Polish was her mother.

Mistress Polish still wanted her daughter, Placentia, to wed a high-ranking man.

Mistress Polish said:

"Oh! May God give you joy, Mademoiselle Compass! You are his whirlpool now, all-to-be-married — thoroughly married — against your mother's permission and without counsel!"

A whirlpool draws everything to itself.

Mistress Polish continued:

"He's fished fair and caught a frog, I fear.

"What fortune do you have to bring him in a marriage portion? What dower do you have? You can tell stories now: You know a world of secrets to reveal."

Pleasance knew about the birth of Placentia's child.

"I know nothing but what is told to me, nor can I discover anything," Pleasance said.

Neither Mistress Polish nor Pleasance (unless Compass had told her, which is possible) knew at this point that Compass had learned that Mistress Polish was not Pleasance's mother.

Mistress Polish said:

"No, you shall not discover anything, I'll take order — I'll take steps to prevent it.

"Go, get you in there. It is Ember Week! I'll keep you fasting from his flesh for a while."

Ember Week was a time of fasting on Wednesday, Friday, and Saturday.

Mistress Polish would keep Pleasance and Compass from consummating their marriage for a while.

Pleasance exited.

"See who's here?" Mother Chair said about Placentia. "She's been with My Lady, who kissed her, all-to-kissed her — thoroughly kissed her — twice or thrice."

"And called her niece again, and viewed her linen," Nurse Keep said.

Placentia's sheets were not bloodstained, as they would have been if she had given birth. Of course, a laundress had been busy.

"You have done a miracle, Mother Chair," Mistress Polish said.

"Not I," Mother Chair said. "My caudle has done it. Thank my caudle heartily."

Her caudle — a medicinal drink — had enabled Placentia to leave her bed and see Lady Loadstone.

Mistress Polish said:

"It shall be thanked, and you, too, wisest Mother.

"You shall have a new, splendid, four-pound beaver hat, set with enameled studs, as mine is here, and a right — genuine — pair of crystal spectacles, crystal of the rock, thou mighty mother of dames, hung in an ivory case at a gold belt, and silver bells to jingle as you pace before your fifty daughters in procession to church, or from the church."

The beaver hat would cost four pounds.

"Crystal of the rock" is transparent quartz.

Mother Chair had been present at the birth of fifty girls: her figurative daughters.

After childbirth women did not go to church for four weeks. The midwife then accompanied them as they went to church again.

"Thanks, Mistress Polish," Mother Chair said.

"She deserves as many pensions as there are pieces in a — maidenhead, if I were a prince to give them," Nurse Keep said.

"Pieces" are coins. They can also be penises.

A maidenhead can be sold. If a young prostitute is a good actress, it can be sold over or over.

Mother Chair deserved a pension for each young unmarried mother whom she helped to be married to a well-born man.

If Placentia can keep up the pretense of being a virgin, she can "sell" her "maidenhead" to a well-born husband.

Mistress Polish said to Placentia, "Come, sweet charge, you shall present yourself about the house. Be confident and bear up. You shall be seen."

People needed to see that Placentia did not look like she had just given birth.

They exited.

153

Compass and Captain Ironside argued with Master Practice.

Compass wanted to make peace with him, but Master Practice was angry because he had wanted to marry Pleasance, but Compass had tricked him.

"What!" Compass said. "I can make you amends, my learnèd counsel, and satisfy a greater injury and violation of rights to chafed, irritated Master Practice. Who would think that you could be thus testy?"

"He has a grave head, given over to the study of our laws!" Captain Ironside said.

"And to the prime honors of the commonwealth," Compass said.

"And he has you to mind a wife," Captain Ironside said.

Compass was focusing his attention on a wife, something that perhaps Master Interest did not have time to do because of his professional interests.

"What should you do with such a toy as a wife who might distract you or hinder you in your career course?" Compass asked.

"He shall not think of it," Captain Ironside said.

Compass said, "I will make over and transfer to you my possession of that same place that has fallen void, you know, to satisfy you: Surveyor of the Projects General."

To make amends with Master Practice, Compass will give him the possession of the office of Surveyor of the Projects General.

"And that's an office you know how to stir in and be busy in," Captain Ironside said.

"And make your profits from," Compass said.

"Profits are, indeed, the ends and objectives of a gowned man — a lawyer such as you," Captain Ironside said. "Show your activity and show how you are built for business."

"I accept it as a possession, even if it is only a reversion," Master Practice said.

A reversion is the right to succeed in the office; when the person who has that office dies, the successor takes possession of the office.

"You were the first who told me it was a possession," Compass said.

Master Practice had told Compass that Thinwit, who held the office of Surveyor of the Projects General, had died. If that was true, the reversion had become a possession.

"Aye, I told you that I heard that," Master Practice said.

"All is one. That doesn't matter," Captain Ironside said. "He'll make reversion a possession quickly."

In other words: Thinwit will die soon, if he isn't already dead, and the reversion will become a possession. Apparently, Thinwit was in the process of dying.

"But I must have a general release from you," Compass said.

A general release would acknowledge that Compass had given Master Practice the right of succession to the office, and so, if for some reason Master Practice did not succeed in obtaining the office, Compass would not be liable.

"Do one; I'll do the other," Master Practice said.

They would write two documents: one for giving away the reversion/possession, and one for the general release.

"It's a match — an agreement — before my brother Ironside," Compass said. "He will be the witness."

"It is done," Master Practice said.

They shook hands.

"We two are reconciled, then," Compass said.

Two more humors had been reconciled.

"To a lawyer who can make use of a place, any half-title is better than a wife," Captain Ironside said.

A half-title is a half-claim. A lawyer would know how to make the best use of it.

"And it will save the expense of coaches, velvet gowns, and cut-work smocks for a wife," Compass said.

Cut-work smocks have open embroidery.

"He is to occupy an office wholly," Captain Ironside said.

The work of the office will entirely fill the lawyer's — Master Practice's — time.

Compass said:

"That is true.

"I must talk with you nearer — about something that affects me more closely, Master Practice. It is about the recovery of my wife's marriage portion, and what course of action I would be best to take to get it from Sir Moth Interest."

"The plainest way," Master Practice said.

"What's that, for plainness?" Compass said.

Master Practice said:

"Sue him at common law.

"Arrest him on an action of choke-bail: five hundred thousand pounds. It will frighten him and all his sureties."

"Choke-bail" is bail that is a huge sum of money and is intended to keep the accused in jail due to inability to raise the bail.

"Sureties" are people who would normally guarantee the bail, but in this case they would balk at being sureties for so large a sum.

Master Practice then asked:

"You can prove your marriage?"

"Yes," Compass said. "We'll talk of it inside, and we will hear what My Lady has to say."

They exited.

Sir Moth Interest and Lady Loadstone talked together.

"I'm sure the brogue of the house went all that way," Sir Moth Interest said. "She was with child, and Master Compass got it."

The brogue is 1) a cheat, and 2) an escheat.

Since Placentia bore an illegitimate child, she was not eligible for the marriage portion, according to Sir Moth Interest. Therefore, the escheat.

Lady Loadstone said:

"Why, that, you see, is manifestly false.

"He's married the other, our true niece, he says. He would not woo them both; he is not such a stallion to leap on and have sex with all.

"Also, no child appears that I can find with all my search and all the strictest inquiry I have made through all my family."

Her "family" included all her household servants.

Lady Loadstone continued:

"A fit of the mother — that is, a fit of hysteria — the women say she had, which the midwife cured with burning bones and feathers."

Doctor Rut entered the scene.

Seeing Doctor Rut coming, Lady Loadstone said:

"Here's the doctor."

Sir Moth Interest said, "Oh, noble doctor, didn't you and your Tim Item tell me that our niece was in labor?"

"If I did, what follows?" Doctor Rut asked.

"And didn't you tell me that Mother Midnight was sent for?" Sir Moth Interest asked.

"Mother Midnight" can be 1) a midwife, or 2) a bawd.

Here, of course, it refers to Mother Chair.

"So she was, and she is in the house still," Doctor Rut said.

"But here has a noise — a rumor — been since, that Placentia was delivered of a brave — a splendid — boy, and it was of Master Compass' begetting," Sir Moth Interest said.

Doctor Rut said:

"I know no rattle of gossips, nor their noises.

"I hope you do not take me for a pimp errant — a wandering, wrong-doing pimp — to deal in smock-affairs."

"Smock-affairs" are women's affairs.

He then asked:

"Where's the patient, the infirm man about whom I was sent for — where's Squire Needle?"

"Is Needle sick?" Lady Loadstone asked.

"My apothecary tells me that he is in danger," Doctor Rut said.

The apothecary, Tim Item, entered the scene.

"How are things, Tim? Where is he?" Doctor Rut asked.

"I cannot hold him down," Tim Item said. "He's up and walks and talks in his perfect sleep with his eyes shut, as sensibly as if he were broad awake. Although he is sound asleep, he appears as if he is in control of his senses."

"Look, here he comes," Sir Moth Interest said, looking up. "He's fast asleep: observe him."

Doctor Rut said, "He'll tell us wonders."

Seeing some women with Master Needle, he asked, "What are these women doing here?"

— 5.5 —

Half-undressed, Master Needle entered the scene. He was followed by Mistress Polish, Mother Chair, Nurse Keep, and Placentia.

"Hunting a man half naked?" Doctor Rut said. "You are fine beagles! You'd have his doucets."

Beagles are a pack of hunting hounds, and doucets are deer testicles.

Master Needle said, "I have linen breeks — breeches — on."

"Breeches" are a kind of underwear.

Master Needle had heard the reference to "doucets," and he was responding to it.

"He hears, but he can see nothing," Doctor Rut said.

Master Needle responded, "Yes, I see who hides the treasure yonder."

"Huh?" Sir Moth Interest said. "What treasure?"

He was interested in treasure.

"If you ask questions, he awakens at once," Doctor Rut said, "and then you'll hear no more until his next fit."

And I see whom she hides it for," Master Needle said.

Doctor Rut said quietly to Sir Moth Interest, "Do you note that, sir? Listen."

"A fine she-spirit it is, an Indian magpie," Master Needle said. "She was an alderman's widow, and she fell in love with our Sir Moth, My Lady's brother."

Indian magpies are literally a species of thieving, acquisitive, hoarding birds. Figuratively, they are ladies with expensive tastes.

Having fallen in love with Sir Moth Interest, the alderman's widow may have left treasure for him.

"Do you hear this?" Doctor Rut said quietly to Sir Moth Interest.

Master Needle said, "And she has hidden an alderman's estate, dropped through her bill in little holes in the garden, and she scrapes earth over them, where none can spy but I, who see all by the glow-worm's light that creeps before."

Birds have beaks, aka bills. Like a bird that gathers and hides bright objects, the alderman's wife had apparently hidden treasure in little holes in the garden.

Glow-worms are lightning bugs, aka fireflies.

Mistress Polish said, "I knew the gentlewoman, Alderman Parrot's widow, a fine speaker as any was in the clothing or the bevy. She did become her scarlet and black velvet, her green and purple —"

Parrots speak without understanding what they say.

The clothing is the distinctive clothing of an alderman's wife, or the livery of a company, and the bevy is a group of ladies.

Doctor Rut interrupted, "— save thy colors, rainbow —"

He then said to Master Needle, "— or she will run thee over, and all thy lights."

In other words: Madame Polish will talk over you and your lungs.

One meaning of "lights" is lungs.

Her talking would interfere with Master Needle's story about hidden treasure, a story that interested Sir Moth Interest, who was present, and which they wanted Sir Moth Interest to hear.

Mistress Polish kept talking:

"She dwelt in Dolittle Lane atop of the hill there in the round cage, which was after — in the style of — Sir Chime Squirrel's. She would eat nothing but almonds, I assure you."

Some rolling cages for squirrels had chiming bells. They are exercise wheels. Small rolling cages are called hamster wheels.

Almonds are a treat for a squirrel.

"I wish thou had a dose of pills, a double dose of the best purge, to make thee turn tale the other way!" Doctor Rut said.

"Tale" sounds like "tail," or posterior. Purging can be done with the mouth through vomiting, or with the posterior through defecation.

Mistress Needle exited, followed by Mother Chair, Nurse Keep, and Placentia.

Mistress Polish, Lady Loadstone, Doctor Rut, Sir Moth Interest, and Tim Item remained behind.

Mistress Polish said to Doctor Rut:

"You are a foul-mouthed, purging, absurd doctor. I tell you true, and I did long to tell it to you.

"You have spread a scandal in My Lady's house here on her sweet niece that you never can take off with all your purges or your plaster of oaths, even if you were to distil your 'damn me' drop by drop in your defense."

A "plaster" is a bandage.

Mistress Polish continued:

"As for your saying that she has had a child, here she spits on thee and defies thee, or I will do it for her."

Doctor Rut said to Lady Loadstone:

"Madam, please bind and constrain her to her behavior.

"Tie your gossip — your companion — up, or send her to Bedlam Hospital for the Insane."

Mistress Polish said:

"Go thou thither, who better has deserved it, shame of doctors!

"Where could she be delivered? By what charm could she be restored to her strength so soon? Who is the father? And where is the infant?

"Ask your oracle — Master Needle — who walks and talks in his sleep."

Doctor Rut said:

"Where is he? Gone?

"You have lost a fortune listening to Mistress Polish, to her tabor."

A tabor is literally a drum, and figuratively, here, a tongue.

The fortune, of course, was the treasure that Master Needle had been talking about as he "walked in his sleep."

Doctor Rut continued:

"Good madam, lock her up."

"You must give losers — those who have lost something — their leave to speak, good doctor," Lady Loadstone said.

A proverb stated, "Give losers leave [permission] to speak."

Doctor Rut said, "Follow his footing — Master Needle's track — before he gets to his bed. This rest is lost else."

Doctor Rut, Sir Moth Interest, and Tim Item exited.

Lady Loadstone and Mistress Polish remained behind.

Compass, Master Practice, and Captain Ironside entered the scene.

"Where is my wife?" Compass asked Mistress Polish. "What have you done with my wife, you gossip of the counsels?"

Mistress Polish was one of the group of people who advised Lady Loadstone.

"I, sweet Master Compass?" Mistress Polish said. "I honor you and your wife."

"Well, do so still," Compass said. "I will not call you mother, though, but Polish. Good Gossip Polish, where have you hidden my wife?"

"I hide your wife?" Mistress Polish said.

"Or she's run away," Compass said.

"That would make all suspected, sir, afresh," Lady Loadstone said.

If Pleasance had run away, that would make people suspicious that she was not in fact Lady Loadstone's niece. It would look as if she were running away because she was guilty of trying to fraudulently get Placentia's marriage portion.

Lady Loadstone continued:

"Come, we will find her, if she is in the house."

"Why should I hide your wife, good Master Compass?" Mistress Polish asked.

"I know no reason except that you are Goody Polish, who is good at malice, good at evil, all that can perplex or trouble a business thoroughly," Compass replied.

"You may say what you will," Mistress Polish said. "You're Master Compass, and you carry a large sweep, sir, in your circle."

The large sweep was a large amount of influence among his friends and associates. It also glanced at a large area made by a compass.

Lady Loadstone said to Mistress Polish:

"I'll sweep all corners, gossip, to spring this, to make it appear out of hiding, if it is above ground."

She meant that she would make Pleasance appear from out of hiding; however, readers know that if things worked out well, she could also make Mistress Polish's secret come out of hiding and be made public.

Lady Loadstone continued:

"I will have her cried by the common crier — the town crier — throughout all the ward, but I will find her."

She would raise a hue and cry of people to set out and find her.

"It will be an act worthy your justice, madam," Captain Ironside said.

"And it will become the integrity, innocence and soundness, and worship of her name," Master Practice said.

Doctor Rut and Sir Moth Interest entered the scene.

"It is such a fly, this gossip," Doctor Rut said about Mistress Polish. "With her buzz, she blows on everything in every place!"

A fly blows — lays eggs — on everything. It makes everything dirty.

Mistress Polish's buzzing and blowing breath had made it difficult to hear the "sleepwalking" Master Needle's words about buried treasure.

Sir Moth Interest said:

"A busy woman is a fearful grievance!"

In other words, a meddlesome woman is a dreadful cause of suffering.

Sir Moth Interest then asked:

"Won't he sleep again?"

Doctor Rut said:

"Yes, quickly, as soon as he is warm. It is the nature of the disease, and all these cold dry fumes that are melancholic, to work at first slowly and insensibly in their ascent from the stomach to the brain, until being got up; and then distilling down upon the brain, they have a pricking, irritating quality that breeds this restless rest (which we, the sons — the followers — of the art of medicine, call a walking in the sleep) and the telling of mysteries and secret knowledge that must be heard — softly, with art, as if we were sewing pillows under the patients' elbows."

According to Doctor Rut, they needed to tend the patient — Master Needle — carefully and quietly and without disturbing him. If they don't disturb the patient, they may be able to hear his story.

Doctor Rut continued:

"If we don't tend the patients gently, then they'd fly into a frenzy, run into the woods, where there are noises, huntings, shoutings, hallowings, amid the brakes and furzes and thickets and shrubs, run over bridges, fall into waters, scratch their flesh, sometimes drop down a precipice, and there be lost."

Tim Item entered the scene.

Seeing him, Doctor Rut asked him:

"How are things now! What is Master Needle doing?"

"He is up again, and he begins to talk," Tim Item said.

"About the former matter, Item?" Sir Moth Interest asked.

"The treasure and the lady: That's his theme — that's what Master Needle talks about," Tim Item said.

"Oh, me, I am a happy — fortunate — man!" Sir Moth Interest said. "He cannot put off talking about it. I shall know all, then."

Doctor Rut said quietly to himself:

"With what appetite and craving our own desires delude us!"

He then said:

"Listen, Tim. Let no man interrupt us."

Tim Item replied, "Sir Diaphanous and Master Bias, his court friends, desire to kiss his niece's hands and rejoice in and congratulate her in the firm recovery of her good fame and honor."

Sir Moth Interest said:

"Good.

"Say to them, Master Item, that my niece, Placentia, is by My Lady's side: they'll find her there.

"I ask to be spared for only half an hour. I'll see them soon."

He wanted to stay and learn about the buried treasure.

Doctor Rut said:

"Do, put them off, Tim, and tell them the importance of the business."

Master Needle entered the scene.

Seeing him, Doctor Rut said:

"Here, he has come, indeed, and we will have all the information out of him!

The "sleepwalking" Master Needle said:

"How do you do, ladybird? So hard at work still?

"What's that you are saying? Do you bid me walk, sweet bird? And tell our knight?

"I will. What? Walk, knave, walk?

"I think you're angry with me, Pol. Fine Pol! Pol's a fine bird! O fine lady Pol! An almond for parrot. Parrot's a brave — a splendid — bird.

"Three hundred thousand pieces have you stuck edge-long into the ground within the garden?

"O bounteous bird!"

"Edge-long" means "on the edge." Doctor Needle is talking about Alderman Parrot's widow placing coins on their edge into the hole.

"And me, most happy creature!" Sir Moth Interest said.

He was very happy indeed.

"Smother your joy!" Doctor Rut said, pretending that he was worried that Sir Moth Interest would wake up Master Needle.

"What?" Master Needle said. "And dropped twice so many —"

"Ha!" Sir Moth Interest said. "Where?"

This was an enormous number of coins: three hundred thousand coins buried, and six hundred thousand pieces dropped.

"Contain yourself," Doctor Rut said to Sir Moth Interest.

"In the old well?" the "sleepwalking" Master Needle asked.

Sir Moth Interest said:

"I cannot contain myself. I am a man of flesh and blood.

"Who can contain himself to hear the ghost of a dead lady do such works as these? And a city lady, too, of the straight waist?"

A city lady with a straight waist was a city lady who was wearing a narrow-fitting corset. She was strait-laced, aka morally upright.

Master Needle started to leave.

"He's gone," Doctor Rut said.

"I will go and test the truth of it," Master Needle said.

One way of testing the truth of what the ghost had said was to look for some of the coins.

He exited.

"Follow him, Tim," Doctor Rut said. "See what he does. See if he brings you assay — a specimen — of it now."

Tim Item exited.

"I'll say he's a rare fellow," Sir Moth Interest said, "and he has a rare disease."

"Rare" can mean 1) splendid, and/or 2) unusual.

"And I will work as rare a cure upon him," Doctor Rut said.

"How, good doctor?" Sir Moth Interest asked.

Doctor Rut answered, "When he has uttered all that you would know from him, I'll cleanse him with a pill as small as a pea and stop his mouth, for there is his issue between the muscles of the tongue."

"His issue" is 1) his medical problem, and/or 2) his words that issue from his mouth.

The human tongue has eight muscles.

Tim Item returned.

"He's come back," Sir Moth Interest said.

"What did he do, Item?" Doctor Rut asked.

"The first step he stepped into the garden, he pulled these five pieces up in a finger's breadth one after another," Tim Item said. "The dirt sticks on them still."

A "piece" is a coin. The five pieces were tightly packed together with little or no room between them.

Sir Moth Interest said:

"I know enough.

"Doctor, proceed with your cure. I'll make thee famous, famous among the sons of the physicians, Machaon, Podalirius, Aesculapius.

Aesculapius is the god of medicine, and Machaon and Podalirius are his sons and also physicians.

Sir Moth Interest continued:

"Thou shall have a golden beard as well as Aesculapius had, and thy Tim Item here shall have one of silver: a livery beard. And so will all thy apothecaries who belong to — who work for — thee."

A statue of Aesculapius at Epidaurus had a golden beard. Dionysius, the tyrant of Syracuse, ordered that the beard be detached.

The apothecaries who work for Doctor Needle would wear a beard made of silver to show that they worked for him. The silver beards would be part of their livery: distinctive clothing that showed for whom they worked.

Sir Moth Interest then asked:

"Where's Squire Needle? Gone?

"He's pricked — gone — away, now he has done the work," Tim Item said.

"Prepare his pill and give it to him before supper," Doctor Rut said.

"I'll send for a dozen laborers tomorrow to turn the surface of the garden up," Sir Moth Interest said.

"In mold?" Doctor Rut said. "Bruise every clod?"

He was asking if the soil would be thoroughly dug up. "Mold" is the top soil of a garden or other cultivated land.

"Clods" can be 1) lumps of dirt, or 2), a blockhead, aka clodpate.

Sir Moth Interest was a clodpate whose foolishness in believing this tale would soon be revealed.

Sir Moth Interest continued, "And I'll have all the soil sifted — for I'll not lose a piece of the bird's bounty — and I'll take an inventory of it all."

He wanted *all* of the buried three hundred thousand coins.

Doctor Rut began, "And then I would go down into the well —"

Sir Moth Interest interrupted, "— myself. No trusting other hands. Add six hundred thousand to the first three, and you have nine hundred thousand pounds —"

Doctor Rut interrupted, "— it will purchase the whole bench of aldermanity stripped to their shirts."

Not only would that amount of money buy all the aldermen, but it would also buy their outer clothing.

Prostitutes were paraded half-naked behind carts as a punishment.

Sir Moth Interest said, "There never did accrue so great a gift to man, and from a lady whom I never saw but once. I remember now that we met at Merchant Taylors Hall at dinner in Threadneedle Street."

This was a place for prestigious entertainment.

"The name of Threadneedle Street was a sign Squire Needle should have the threading of this thread," Doctor Rut said.

"That is true," Sir Moth Interest said. "I shall love parrots better while I know him."

"I'd have her statue cut now in white marble," Doctor Rut said.

"And have it painted in most orient — brilliant — colors," Sir Moth Interest said.

"That's right!" Doctor Rut said. "All city statues must be painted; otherwise, they are worth nothing in their subtle and cunning judgments."

The city aldermen are capable of being bribed. In order for their subtle and cunning — and unethical — judgments to be regarded in a good light, the alderman must be painted. That is, they must be misrepresented — they must be given a false coloring.

Statues in ancient Greece and Rome were painted, but Sir Henry Wotton called the painting of statues "an English barbarism" in his *The Elements of Architecture* (1624).

Master Bias entered the scene.

"My truest friend in court, dear Master Bias!" Sir Moth Interest said. "Have you heard of the recovery of our niece in fame and reputation?"

"Yes, I have been with her and congratulated her and rejoiced with her, but I am sorry to find the author of the foul aspersion here in your company," Master Bias said. "I mean this insolent doctor."

Sir Moth Interest replied:

"You are mistaken about him. He is clear got off on it: He is not responsible for it. A gossip's jealousy first gave the hint. He drives and goes another way now, the way that I would have him go.

"He's a rare man, the doctor, in his way. He's done the noblest cure here in the house on a poor squire, my sister's tailor, Master Needle, who talked in his sleep and who would walk to St. John's Wood and Waltham Forest, escape by all the ponds and pits in the way, run over two-inch-wide bridges with his eyes fast asleep and eyelids shut fast and in the dead of night!"

Sir Moth Interest continued:

"I'll have you better acquainted with him."

He then said to Doctor Rut:

"Doctor, here is my dear, dear, dearest friend in court, wise, powerful Master Bias. I ask that you salute each other, not as strangers, but true friends."

"Is this the gentleman you brought today to be a suitor to your niece?" Doctor Rut asked.

"Yes," Sir Moth Interest answered.

"You made an agreement I heard," Doctor Rut said. "Has the written agreement been drawn up between you?"

"And sealed and notarized," Sir Moth Interest said.

"What broke you off?" Doctor Rut asked.

"This rumor about her, about Placentia, wasn't it, Master Bias?" Sir Moth Interest asked.

"Which I find now false and therefore I have come to make amends in the first place," Master Bias said. "I stand to — insist on — the old conditions."

Doctor Rut said, "In faith, give them to him, Sir Moth, whatever they were. You have a brave, splendid occasion now to cross and thwart the flaunting, haughty show-off Master Compass, who pretends to have the right to the marriage portion by the other entail."

An entail is a right to an inheritance.

"And he claims it," Sir Moth Interest said. "You have heard that he's married?"

Master Bias replied:

"We hear that his wife has run away from him, inside.

"She is not to be found in the house, despite all the hue and cry that is made for her through every room.

"The larders have been searched, the bake-houses, and bolting-tub, the ovens, the wash-house and the brew-house, indeed, the very furnace, and yet she is not heard of."

Larders are places for storing food.

A bolting-tub is a tub in which bran is sifted from grain.

A furnace is an oven.

Sir Moth Interest said:

"May she never again be heard of. The safety of Great Britain lies not on it."

In other words: Pleasance is not important; the safety of Great Britain does not rest on her.

Sir Moth Interest continued:

"You are content with the ten thousand pounds, and with defalking — deducting — the four hundred pounds garnish money?"

The garnish money was for expenses: the expenses of fine clothing and whatever was necessary to impress Lady Loadstone and Placentia.

Sir Moth Interest continued:

"That's the condition here, before the doctor, and that's your demand, friend Bias?"

"It is, Sir Moth," Master Bias said.

Parson Palate entered the scene.

"Here comes the parson, then, who shall make the agreement all sure and secure," Doctor Rut said.

"Go with my friend Bias, Parson Palate, to my niece, Placentia," Sir Moth Interest said. "Assure them — witness their engagement — we are in agreement about the wedding."

"And Mistress Compass — Pleasance — too, is found inside," Parson Palate said.

"Where was she hidden?" Sir Moth Interest asked.

"In an old bottle-house where they scraped trenchers; there her mother had thrust her," Parson Palate said.

A bottle-house is a place for storing bottles of ale and wine.

Trenchers are plates, often wooden.

"You shall have time, sir, to triumph on Compass when this fine feat is done, and to triumph on his Rud Ironside," Doctor Rut said.

They exited.

Compass, Pleasance (now Mistress Compass), Lady Loadstone, Captain Ironside, Master Practice, Mistress Polish, Mother Chair, and Nurse Keep met together. A few servants were present.

Compass said, "Was any gentlewoman ever used so barbarously by a malicious gossip, pretending and claiming to be the mother to her, too?"

Mistress Polish had treated Pleasance badly by pretending to be her mother. She had deprived Pleasance of the knowledge that Lady Loadstone was her aunt, and she had attempted — and was still attempting — to get Pleasance's marriage portion and to have it benefit Placentia.

"Pretending and claiming!" Mistress Polish said. "Sir, I am her mother, and I challenge — I assert that I have — a right and legal power and authority for what I have done."

Compass said:

"Out, hag! Out, witch! Out, thou who have put all nature off and behaved unnaturally, and who have put off women's nature!

"For sordid, foul, corrupt gain, thou betrayed the trust committed to thee by the dead, just as you betrayed the trust from the living, and thou exchanged the poor innocent infants in their cradles.

"For sordid, foul, corrupt gain, thou defrauded them of their parent.

"For sordid, foul, corrupt gain, thou changed their names, calling Placentia 'Pleasance,' and calling Pleasance 'Placentia.'"

Not only had the babies been exchanged, but their names had also been exchanged.

To avoid confusion, this book will continue to use the name "Placentia" for the woman who has hitherto been called Placentia, and this book will continue to use the name "Pleasance" for the woman who has hitherto been called Pleasance. The only exception will be when a varlet refers to Compass' wife as Placentia.

Madame Polish whispered to Nurse Keep, "How does he know this?"

Compass continued:

"For sordid, foul, corrupt gain, thou abused and did wrong to the neighborhood.

"But most of all thou abused this lady; thou did force this poor woman" — he pointed to Nurse Keep — "to make an oath on a pious book that she would keep close and secret thy impiety towards her child: Pleasance."

The lady who was abused was Lady Loadstone, whose child was Pleasance.

Mistress Polish whispered to Nurse Keep, "Have you told this to Compass?"

"I told it?" Nurse Keep whispered. "No, he knows it, and much more, as he's a cunning-man."

"A cunning fool, if that is all," Mistress Polish whispered.

So far, Compass had made allegations but had produced no evidence.

Compass said, "But now let's turn to your true daughter, Placentia, who had the child and who is the proper Pleasance. We must have an account of that, too, gossip."

Earlier, readers learned that when Mistress Polish had exchanged the two babies, she had also exchanged their names, calling Placentia "Pleasance," and calling Pleasance "Placentia."

Therefore, the woman who has been called "Placentia" is actually Pleasance. And therefore, Mistress Compass' real name is Placentia.

"This is like all the rest of Master Compass," Mistress Polish said.

Again, so far, Compass had made allegations but had produced no evidence.

Doctor Rut ran into the room and shouted:

"Help! Help, for charity!

"Sir Moth Interest has fallen into the well."

"Where? Where?" Lady Loadstone asked.

"In the garden," Doctor Rut said.

Lady Loadstone exited, followed by Captain Ironside.

Doctor Rut then said, "We need a rope to save his life!"

"How did he come to be there?" Compass asked.

"He thought to take possession of a fortune, there newly dropped for him, and the old chain broke, and he, in the bucket, fell down into the well," Doctor Rut said.

"Is it deep?" Compass asked.

"We cannot tell," Doctor Rut said. "A rope — help with a rope!"

Sir Diaphanous Silkworm, Captain Ironside, Tim Item, Master Needle, and a wet Sir Moth Interest entered the scene.

"He has gotten out again," Sir Diaphanous Silkworm said. "The knight has been saved."

"A little soused — drenched — in the water," Captain Ironside said. "Master Needle saved him."

"The water saved him," Tim Item said. "It was a fair and fortunate escape."

He had fallen into water instead of hitting ground.

Master Needle asked Sir Moth Interest, "Are you hurt?"

"I'm a little wet," Sir Moth Interest said.

"That's nothing," Master Needle said.

Doctor Rut said to Sir Moth Interest, "I wished you to wait, sir, until tomorrow, and I told you that it was not a lucky hour; since six o'clock all stars were retrograde."

In other words: The astrological signs were unfavorable after six o'clock.

"In the name of fate or folly, how did you come to be in the bucket?" Lady Loadstone asked.

Sir Moth Interest said:

"That is a *quaere* of another time, sister."

In other words: That is a query to be answered at another time.

He still believed in the treasure's existence.

Sir Moth Interest continued:

"The doctor will resolve you and tell you about why — the doctor who has done the admirablest cure upon your Needle!

"Give me thy hand, good Needle. Thou came timely — at a good time — to rescue me. Take off my hood and coat. And let me shake myself a little to throw the water off me.

"I have a world — a vast quantity — of business."

He still thought that he had nine hundred thousand pieces of business to do.

Sir Moth Interest continued:

"Where is my nephew Bias? And where is his wife?"

Master Bias, Placentia, and Parson Palate entered the scene.

Sir Moth Interest continued:

"Who bids God give them joy? Here they both stand as surely affianced — engaged to be married — as the parson or words can tie them."

Master Bias and Placentia were not technically married, although Parson Palate had witnessed a betrothal ceremony between them.

"We all wish them joy and happiness," Doctor Rut said.

"I saw the contract and can witness it," Sir Diaphanous Silkworm said.

"He shall receive ten thousand pounds tomorrow," Sir Moth Interest said. "You looked for and expected to get that amount of money, Compass, or a greater sum, but it is disposed of, this is, another way. I have but one niece, truly, Compass."

"I'll find another niece for you," Compass said.

A varlet entered the scene.

"Varlet, do your duty," Compass said.

A varlet is an official who has the power to arrest people.

The varlet said, "I arrest your body, Sir Moth Interest, in the king's name, at the instigation of Master Compass and Dame Placentia, his wife. The action's legally entered into the register. Five hundred thousand pounds is the bail."

Mistress Compass' real name (the name given at birth) was Placentia; however, to avoid confusion, this book will continue to use the name

"Pleasance" for the woman who has hitherto been called Pleasance and who is now Mistress Compass.

"Do you hear this, sister?" Sir Moth Interest asked. "And has your house the ears to hear it, too? And to resound the affront?"

"I cannot stop the laws or hinder justice," Lady Loadstone said. "I can be your bail, if it may be taken."

Compass said, "With the captain's, I ask no better."

Compass was willing for Lady Loadstone and Captain Ironside to be sureties — guarantors — for Sir Moth Interest's bail.

"Here are better men who will give their bail," Doctor Rut said.

Compass said:

"But yours will not be taken, worshipful doctor. You are good security for a suit of clothes to the tailor who dares to trust you, but not for such a sum as is this action."

People often owed tailors much money, but that amount of money would not come close to the sum needed now for bail: five hundred thousand pounds.

Compass then said, "Varlet, you know my mind."

The varlet said to Sir Moth Interest, "You must go to prison, sir, unless you can find bail the creditor likes and is willing to accept as security."

"I would eagerly find it, if you'd show me where," Sir Moth Interest said.

Of course, Sir Moth Interest still believed that nine hundred coins were buried in the garden and dropped into the well.

"It is a terrible action, more indeed than many a man is worth," Sir Diaphanous Silkworm said. "And it is called fright-bail."

Captain Ironside said:

"In faith, I will bail him at my own apperil — my own risk.

"Varlet, begone. Go now."

The varlet exited.

Captain Ironside continued:

"I'll for this once have the reputation to be security for such a sum.

"Bear up, Sir Moth."

Doctor Rut said to himself, "He is not worth the buckles about his belt, and yet this Ironside clashes."

A saying of the time about a worthless person was that he was "not worth two shoe buckles."

Captain Ironside was clashing: making a loud noise as of a soldier in combat.

Sir Moth Interest said quietly to Doctor Rut:

"Be quiet, lest he hear you, doctor. We'll make use of him."

Dionysus, the same tyrant of Syracuse who ordered that the golden beard of Aesculapius be detached from his statue, once said after seizing some gold and silver tablets from temples dedicated to the good gods, "Through their goodness we will make use of them."

Captain Ironside had just volunteered to be a guarantor of Sir Moth Interest's bail.

Sir Moth Interest then said to Captain Ironside:

"What does your brother Compass, Captain Ironside, demand of us by way of challenge thus?"

In other words: Why did Compass have me arrested? And what does he want?

"Your niece's marriage portion, in the right of his wife," Captain Ironside said.

Sir Moth Interest said:

"I have assured one marriage portion to one niece, and I have no more nieces to account for that I know of.

"What I may do in charity, if my sister will bid — ask for — an offering for her maid and him as a benevolent act of charity to them after supper, I'll spit into the basin and entreat my friends to do the like."

A wedding tradition was for guests to put gifts into a basin.

Compass replied:

"Spit out thy gall and heart, thou viper; I will now show no mercy, no pity of thee, thy false niece, and Needle."

He then said to Placentia:

"Bring forth your child, or I will appeal you — I will accuse you — of murder, you, and this gossip here, and Mother Chair."

He was referring to Placentia, Mistress Polish, and Mother Chair.

"The gentleman's fallen mad!" Mother Chair said.

Mother Chair was still denying that there was a baby.

Pleasance stepped forward and said:

"No, Mistress Midwife. I saw the child, and you did give it to me and put it in my arms; by this ill token, this evil token, you wished me such another, and it cried."

Mother Chair wanted Pleasance either 1) to give birth to a healthy baby, or 2) to give birth to a bastard.

"The law is plain," Master Practice said. "If it were heard to cry and you do not produce it, he may indict all who conceal it of felony and murder."

A cry indicated a live birth, not a stillbirth.

Infanticide is murder. Being an accessary before or after the fact is a felony.

Hiding a pregnancy was also a crime.

"And I will take the boldness, sir, to do it," Compass said, "beginning with Sir Moth here and his doctor."

He was accusing them of hiding the pregnancy and perhaps worse.

"In good faith, this same is like to turn a business," Sir Diaphanous Silkworm said.

It was likely to become a source of great trouble and distress.

People could lose their lives, not just money and reputation.

"And a shrewd, dangerous business, by the Virgin Mary," Parson Palate said. "They all start at it. It makes them afraid."

Compass said:

"I have the right thread now, I'm on the right path, and I will keep on it.

"You, Goody Keep, confess the truth to My Lady, the truth, the whole truth, and nothing but the truth."

Mistress Polish said:

"I scorn to be prevented — deprived — of my glories and achievements. I will acknowledge what I have done.

"I plotted the deceit, and I will own up to it. Love to my child and lucre — money — gained from the marriage portion provoked and motivated me; wherein, although the eventual outcome has failed in part, I will make use of the best side."

She would look on the bright side.

"This" — she pointed to Placentia — "is my daughter, and she has had a child this day — to her shame, I now profess and confess it — by this mere false-stick Squire Needle."

Squire Needle is a false-stick because his "stick" made Placentia pregnant, but he did not marry her.

Mistress Polish continued:

"But since this wise knight — Sir Moth Interest — has thought it good to change the foolish father of it by assuring — making sure of by engaging — her to his dear friend, Master Bias, and him again to her by clapping of him — making a bargain with him and clapping him on the back — with his free promise of ten thousand pounds, before so many witnesses —"

Mistress Polish was certain that Master Bias and Placentia would be married. There were witnesses that they were engaged to be married. Although Placentia's true identity had been revealed, Mistress Polish thought that the marriage would occur because Placentia needed a husband and Master Bias wanted the ten thousand pounds that Sir Moth Interest had agreed to pay him in front of witnesses.

"Whereof I am one witness," Sir Diaphanous Silkworm said.

"And I am another witness," Parson Palate said.

Mistress Polish said:

"I would be unnatural to my own flesh and blood, if I would not thank him."

She said to Sir Moth Interest:

"I thank you, sir, and I have reason for it.

"For here your true niece stands, fine Mistress Compass — I'll tell you the truth, you have deserved it from me — fine Mistress Compass to whom you are by bond engaged to pay the sixteen thousand pounds that is her portion, due to her husband on her marriage-day.

"I speak the truth, and nothing but the truth."

"You'll pay it now, Sir Moth, with interest?" Captain Ironside said. "You see the truth breaks out on every side of you."

"Into what nets of cozenage and trickery am I cast on every side!" Sir Moth Interest said. "Each thread has grown into a noose, a very mesh. I have run myself into a double brake — snare, trap — of paying twice the money."

As things now stood, he would be paying money out twice, but not the same amount of money each time.

"You shall be released from paying me a penny, with these conditions," Master Bias said.

"Will you leave her, Placentia, then?" Mistress Polish asked.

"Yes, and I will leave the sum twice told, before I take a wife to pick out — to unpick — Monsieur Needle's basting threads," Master Bias said.

"Basting" is "loosely sewed."

Placentia had been loosely sowed. Master Needle had made her pregnant, but he had had no intention of being her husband or being a father to the child.

"Basting" is a procedure to keep meat moist.

"Basting threads" may be streams of semen.

"Basting" also means to pad a garment. Placentia's belly had acquired padding.

"Picking out Monsieur Needle's basting threads" may mean that marrying Placentia would ensure that Master Needle will no longer engage in basting Placentia. Master Bias, however, did not care what happened to Placentia.

Compass said to Mistress Polish:

"Gossip, you are paid.

"Although he is a fit nature, worthy to have a whore justly put on him, he is not bad enough to take your daughter on such a cheating trick."

Mistress Polish had gotten a fit reward: Master Bias would not marry her daughter, and so there would be no husband and no ten thousand pounds for her.

Compass then asked Sir Moth Interest:

"Will you pay the marriage portion now?"

"What will you 'bate?" Sir Moth Interest asked.

"Not a penny the law gives me," Compass said.

"Yes, Bias' money," Sir Moth Interest said.

Compass responded:

"Who? Your friend in court?

"I will not rob you of him, nor the purchase, nor your dear doctor here."

Compass would not rob Sir Moth Interest — take away from him — Master Bias. He also would not rob — take away from him — what he had bought: Master Bias' influence at court. He also would not rob — take away from him — the credit for what he had bought.

Nor would he take away from him Doctor Rut.

Sir Moth Interest had paid Master Bias four hundred pounds to be his friend at court. This was a bribe with which he had purchased Master Bias.

Compass would not take away the credit for that purchase by providing Sir Moth Interest with four hundred pounds from Pleasance's marriage portion.

Compass continued:

"All of you stand all together —

"Birds of a nature all, and of a feather."

A proverb stated, "Birds of a feather flock together."

Lady Loadstone said:

"Well, we are all now reconciled to truth."

In other words: All humors are now reconciled.

She continued:

"There rests yet a gratuity — a gift — from me to be conferred upon this gentleman" — she pointed to Captain Ironside — "who, as my nephew Compass says, was the cause, first of the offence, but since of all the amends."

Compass was now her nephew-in-law because he was married to her niece.

Lady Loadstone continued:

"The quarrel caused the fright; that fright brought on the travail, which made peace; and then the peace drew on this new discovery, which ends all in reconcilement."

The fright had caused Placentia to give birth.

"It ends in reconcilement when the marriage portion has been tendered — handed over — and received," Compass said.

"Well, you must have it, as good do it at first as last," Sir Moth Interest said.

He would hand over the marriage portion quickly.

Lady Loadstone said:

"It is well said, brother.

"And I, if this good captain will accept me, give him myself in marriage, endow him with my estate, and make him lord of me and all my fortunes. He who has saved my honor, though by chance, I'll really study his honor and learn how best to thank him."

"And I embrace you, lady, and your goodness," Captain Ironside said, "and I vow to quit all thought of war hereafter, except what is fought under your colors and for your sake, madam."

He would retire from being a soldier.

"More work then for the parson! I shall cap the Loadstone with an Ironside, I see," Parson Palate said.

"Cap" can mean "cover." In this context, it can mean the missionary sexual position.

Magnets attract iron.

What about Placentia and her baby?

Captain Ironside said:

"And I will take in these, the forlorn, wretched couple, with us, Needle and his thread — Placentia — whose marriage portion I will think about, as being a piece of business waiting on my bounty and generosity.

"Thus I do take possession of you, madam Loadstone, who are my true magnetic and attractive mistress and My Lady."

— CHORUS 5, AND EPILOGUE —

CHORUS 5, changed into an epilogue to the King

John Trygust stepped forward, away from Probee and Damplay, and said to them:

"Well, gentlemen, I now must, under seal

"And the author's charge, waive you [put you aside] and make my appeal

"To the supremest power, My Lord the King,

"Who best can judge of what we humbly bring.

"He knows our [the actors'] weakness and the poet's [playwright's] faults,

"Where he [Ben Jonson] doth [does] stand upright, go firm, or halts [limps],

"And he [the King] will doom [judge] him. To [In deference to] which voice he stands [Ben Jonson submits],

"And prefers [values] that 'fore [before, or instead of] all the people's hands [applause, or lack of it]."

strokes the gills 20
  (1.2.20)
  Source of Above:
  The Cambridge Edition of the Works of Ben Jonson
  7 Volume Set. Volume 2.
  Ben Jonson (Author), David Bevington (Editor), Martin Butler (Editor), Ian Donaldson (Editor).
  Cambridge University Press, 2012. Print. P. 427.
  Wikipedia defines "Trout tickling":

> **Trout tickling** *is the art of rubbing the underbelly of a trout with fingers. If done properly, the trout will go into a trance after a minute or so, and can then easily be retrieved and thrown onto the nearest bit of dry land.*

Source of Above: "Trout tickling." Wikipedia. Accessed 13 June 2022
https://en.wikipedia.org/wiki/Trout_tickling
Wikipedia quotes a 1901 book detailing the practice:

> *Thomas Martindale's 1901 book, Sport, Indeed, describes the method used on trout in the River Wear in County Durham:*

> *The fish are watched working their way up the shallows and rapids. When they come to the shelter of a ledge or a rock it is their nature to slide under it and rest. The poacher sees the edge of a fin or the moving tail, or maybe he sees neither; instinct, however, tells him a fish ought to be there, so he takes the water very slowly and carefully and stands up near the spot. He then kneels on one knee and passes his hand, turned with fingers up, deftly under the rock until it comes in contact with the fish's tail. Then he begins tickling with his forefinger, gradually running his hand along the fish's belly further and further toward the head until it is under the gills. Then comes a quick grasp, a struggle, and the prize*

is wrenched out of his natural element, stunned with a blow on the head, and landed in the pocket of the poacher.

Source of Above: "Trout tickling." Wikipedia. Accessed 13 June 2022
https://en.wikipedia.org/wiki/Trout_tickling
Look up "Trout Tickling" on YouTube. Here is one video:

Trout Tickling on the Elk River (YouTube)

Is trout tickling real? Has it ever really been done? Watch the video taken on the Elk River near Fernie BC in September 2008 and you decide!

https://www.youtube.com/watch?v=tszDNiPqm5c&t=66s

— 1.4 —

RUT

> *Not very well. She cannot shoot at butts,*
> *Or manage a great horse, but she can crunch*
> *A sack of small coal, eat you lime and hair, 15*
> *Soap-ashes, loam, and has a dainty spice*
> *O'the green sickness.*

(1.4.13-17)

Source of Above:

The Cambridge Edition of the Works of Ben Jonson. Volume 2. P. 431-432.

"Green sickness" is hypochemic anemia.

Here is some information from the article "Hypochemic anemia" on Wikipedia:

> **Hypochromic anemia** *is a generic term for any type of anemia in which the red blood cells are paler than normal. (Hypo- refers to less, and chromic means colour.) A normal red blood cell has a biconcave disk shape and will have an area of pallor in its center when viewed microscopically. In hypochromic cells, this area of central pallor is increased. This decrease in redness is due to a disproportionate reduction of red cell hemoglobin (the pigment that imparts the red color) in proportion to the volume of the cell. Clinically the color can be evaluated by the mean corpuscular hemoglobin (MCH) or mean corpuscular hemoglobin concentration (MCHC). The MCHC is considered the better parameter of the two as it adjusts for effect the size of the cell has on its amount of hemoglobin. Hypochromia is clinically defined as below the normal MCH reference range of 27–33 picograms/cell in adults or below the normal MCHC reference range of 33–36 g/dL in adults.*

> *Red blood cells will also be small (microcytic), leading to substantial overlap with the category of microcytic anemia. The most common causes of this kind of anemia are iron deficiency and thalassemia.*

*Hypochromic anemia was historically known as **chlorosis** or **green sickness** for the distinct skin tinge sometimes present in patients, in addition to more general symptoms such as a lack of energy, shortness of breath, dyspepsia, headaches, a capricious or scanty appetite and amenorrhea.*

[...]

Historical understanding

[...]

In 1554, German physician Johannes Lange described a condition, which he called "the disease of virgins" because, he said, it was "peculiar to virgins". The symptoms were wide-ranging, including an appearance which is "pale, as if bloodless", an aversion to food (especially meat), difficulty in breathing, palpitations and swollen ankles. He prescribed that sufferers should "live with men and copulate. If they conceive, they will recover." The symptom picture overlaps to some extent with an earlier condition described in English medical texts, "the green sickness", which was a form of jaundice. However, Lange shifted the cause from digestive errors to the sufferer remaining a virgin, despite being of the age for marriage. The name "chlorosis" was coined in 1615 by Montpellier professor of medicine Jean Varandal from the ancient Greek word "chloros" meaning "greenish-yellow", "pale green", "pale", "pallid" or "fresh". Both Lange and Varandal claimed Hippocrates as a reference, but their lists of symptoms do not match that in the Hippocratic Disease of Virgins, a treatise that was translated into Latin in the 1520s and thus became available to early modern Europe.

In addition to "green sickness", the condition was known as morbus virgineus ("virgin's disease") or febris amatoria ("lover's fever"). Francis Grose's 1811 Dictionary of the Vulgar Tongue defined "green sickness" as: "The disease of maids occasioned by celibacy."

Source of Above: "Hypochemic anemia." Wikipedia. Accessed 15 June 2022.

https://en.wikipedia.org/wiki/Hypochromic_anemia

— 2.3 —

A wind bomb's in her belly

(2.3.20)

Source of Above:

The Cambridge Edition of the Works of Ben Jonson. Volume 2. P. 450.

The below is from David Bruce's book *The Funniest People in Families: Volume 2*:

> Senator Chauncey Depew once made fun of President William Taft's obesity by looking at his waistline, then saying, "I hope, if it is a girl, Mr. Taft will name it for his charming wife." President Taft overheard him and replied, "If it is a girl, I shall, of course, name it for my lovely helpmate of many years. And if it is a boy, I shall claim the father's prerogative and name it Junior. But if, as I suspect, it is only a bag of wind, I shall name it Chauncey Depew."

Source of Above: Retold from Nancy McPhee, *The Second Book of Insults*, pp. 21-22.

— 2.6 —

COMPASS

He may entail a jest upon his house, though,

Enter IRONSIDE.

Or leave a tale to his posterity

To be told after him.

(2.6.102-104)

Source of Above:

The Cambridge Edition of the Works of Ben Jonson. Volume 2. P. 462.

Both rich and poor people can makes jests with their wills or leave a good story:

Source of the Harry Lehr, aka America's Court Jester story in 2.6: Retold from H. Allen Smith, *The Compleat Practical Joker* (New York: Pocket Books, 1956), p. 199.

Source of the John Custis story in 2.6: Retold from Helen Chappell, *The Chesapeake Book of the Dead*, p. 12.

Other Stories:

• In a Cambridge, Massachusetts, cemetery is a funeral monument raised to TRUTH. Jonathan Mann (1821-1892) was a superintendent of the cemetery. He got into a disagreement about how some funds should be spent and took the matter to court, where he lost. Believing that TRUTH was dead, he had a funeral monument raised in her memory.

Source of Above: Retold from Robert E. Pike, *Granite Laughter and Marble Tears*, p. 70.

• On his deathbed, Heinrich Heine made a will that left everything to his wife, Mathilda — provided that she remarry. Why? Mr. Heine

190

explained, "When Mathilda remarries, there will be at least one man who regrets my death."

Source of Above: Retold from Lore and Maurice Cowan, *The Wit of the Jews*, p. 43.

• An epitaph in a cemetery near Stockton, Somerset County, Maryland, said, "You wouldn't come to see me / When I was alive / Don't come to see me / Now that I'm dead."

Source of Above: Retold from Helen Chappell, *The Chesapeake Book of the Dead*, p. 67.

— Chorus 2 —

BOY

They are no other but narrow and shrunk natures, shrivelled up poor things that cannot think well of themselves, who dare to detract others. That signature is upon them, and it will last. A half-witted barbarism which no barber's art or his balls will ever expunge or take out!

(Chorus 2, lines 37-40)

Source of Above:

The Cambridge Edition of the Works of Ben Jonson. Volume 2. P. 467.

Below are two epigrams (bold added) by Martial that mention Cinnamus:

Martial, *Epigrams.* Book 6. Bohn's Classical Library (1897)

LXIV. TO A DETRACTOR.

Although you are neither sprung from the austere race of the Fabii, nor are such as he whom the wife of Curius Dentatus brought forth when seized with her pains beneath a shady oak, as she was carrying her husband his dinner at the plough; but are the son of a father who plucked the hair from his face at a looking-glass, and of a mother condemned to wear the toga in public; [1] *and are one whom your wife might call wife;* [2] *you allow yourself to find fault with my books, which are known to fame, and to carp at my best jokes,——jokes to which the chief men of the city and of the courts do not disdain to lend an attentive ear,———jokes which the immortal Silius deigns to receive in his library, which the eloquent Regulus so frequently repeats, and which win the praises of Sura, the neighbour of the Aventine Diana, who beholds at less distance than others the contests of the great circus.* [3] *Even Caesar himself the lord of all, the supporter of so great a weight of empire, does not think it beneath him to read my jests two or three times. But you, perhaps, have more genius; you have, by the polishing of Minerva, an understanding more acute; and the subtle Athena has formed your taste. May I die, if there is not far more understanding in the heart of the animal which, with entrails hanging down, and large foot, lungs coloured with concealed blood,——an object to be feared by all noses,——is carried by the cruel butcher from street to street You have the audacity, too, to write verses, which no one will read, and to waste your miserable paper upon me.* **But if the heat of my wrath should burn a mark upon you, it will live, and remain, and will be noted all through the city; nor will even Cinnamus, with all his cunning, efface the stigma.** *But have pity upon yourself, and do not, like a furious dog, provoke with rabid mouth the fuming nostrils of a living bear. However calm he may be, and however gently he may lick your fingers and hands, he will, if resentment and bite and just anger excite him, prove a true bear. Let me advise you, therefore, to exercise your teeth on an empty hide, and to seek for carrion which you may bite with impunity.*

Source of Above:
Martial, *Epigrams*. Book 6. Bohn's Classical Library (1897)
https://www.tertullian.org/fathers/martial_epigrams_book06.htm

***

Martial, Epigrams. Book 7. Bohn's Classical Library (1897)
LXIV. TO CINNAMUS.

You, Cinnamus, who were a barber well known over all the city, *and afterwards, by the kindness of your mistress, made a knight, have taken refuge among the cities of Sicily and the regions of Aetna, fleeing from the stern justice of the forum. By what art will you now, useless log, sustain your years? How is your unhappy and fleeting tranquillity to employ itself? You cannot be a rhetorician, a grammarian, a school-master, a Cynic, or Stoic philosopher, nor can you sell your voice to the people of Sicily, or your applause to theatres of Some. All that remains for you, Cinnamus, is to become a barber again.*

Source of Above: Martial, Epigrams. Book 7. Bohn's Classical Library (1897)
https://www.tertullian.org/fathers/martial_epigrams_book07.htm

The below information comes from the Wikipedia article on "Barber's pole":

> *During medieval times, barbers performed surgery on customers, as well as tooth extractions. The original pole had a brass wash basin at the top (representing the vessel in which leeches were kept) and bottom (representing the basin that received the blood). The pole itself represents the staff that the patient gripped during the procedure to encourage blood flow. (and the twined pole motif is likely related to the Staff of Hermes, aka the Caduceus, evidenced for example by early physician van Helmont's of himself as "Francis Mercurius Van Helmont, A Philosopher by that one in whom are all things, A Wandering Hermite," op. cit., preface.)*

Source of Above: "Barber pole." Wikipedia. Accessed 20 June 2022 < https://en.wikipedia.org/wiki/Barber%27s_pole >.

A note in the Cambridge Ben Jonson states:

> ***balls*** *i.e. of soap. Cf. Epicene, 3.5.59-60: during the cursing of Cutbeard, the barber, Truewit suggests 'if he would swallow all his balls for pills, let them not purge him'. Soap was apparently ingested as an emetic.*

Source of Above:
The Cambridge Edition of the Works of Ben Jonson. Volume 2. P. 467.

For Your Information: John Hunter lived much later than Ben Johnson's time, but apparently leeches were sometimes applied to testicles during bloodletting:

> *John Hunter, the founder of modern surgery, advocated the use of bloodletting in his 1794 treatise for the treatment of apoplexy and inflammation.4 He believed that in some cases bleeding could be effective in treating smallpox. For gonorrhea, he recommended the application of leeches to the scrotum and testicles.*

Source of Above: Timothy M. Bell, MLS (ASCP)CM, "A Brief History of Bloodletting." For the Edward Hand Medical Heritage Foundation. *The Journal of Lancaster General Hospital* • Winter 2016 • Vol. 11 – No. 4.

http://www.jlgh.org/JLGH/media/Journal-LGH-Media-Library/Past%20Issues/Volume%2011%20-%20Issue%204/Bloodletting.pdf

For Your Information: "How to Make 16th Century Soap."

Cassidy Cash: "Experience Shakespeare: How to Make 16th Century Soap." YouTube. 9 February 2019

https://www.youtube.com/watch?v=C-LuyRfEyfs

Also for Your Information: "16th Century Soap Recipes."

Since hard soap can be shredded and reformed soap balls came into being, a luxury product used by the upper classes. In Tudor times botanicals were introduced into soap, and scented soap became a "must-have" item of the elite. Fine soaps were produced in Europe from the 16th century on, and many of these soaps are still produced, both industrially and by small-scale artisans. Castile soap is a popular example of the vegetable-only soaps evolved from the oldest "white soap" of Italy. This hard white soap would be grated and used to make specially scented and herbed soap balls/ wash balls.

Source of Above: "16th Century Soap Recipes." La Bella Donna: History is Beautiful. WordPress.

Posted on January 30, 2018 by Fleur-de-Gigi.

https://fleurtyherald.wordpress.com/2018/01/30/16th-century-soap-recipes/

— 3.1 —

KEEP

I have a month's mind
To peep a little, too.
(3.1.23-24)
Source of Above:
The Cambridge Edition of the Works of Ben Jonson. Volume 2. P. 470.

The below information comes from the 1911 *Encyclopædia Britannica* article on "Month's Mind":

MONTH'S MIND, *in medieval and later England a service and feast held one month after the death of anyone in his or her memory. Bede speaks of the day as commemorationis dies. These "Minding days" were of great antiquity, and were survivals of the Norse minne or ceremonial drinking to the dead. "Minnying Days," says Blount, "from the Saxon Lemynde, days which our ancestors called their Monthes mind, their Year's mind and the like, being the days whereon their souls (after their deaths) were had in special remembrance, and some office or obsequies said for them, as Orbits, Dirges." The phrase is still used in Lancashire. Elaborate instructions for the conduct of the commemorative service were often left in wills. Thus, one Thomas Windsor (who died in 1479) orders that "on my moneth's minde there be a hundred children within the age of sixteen years, to say for my soul," and candles were to be burned before the rood in the parish church and twenty priests were to be paid by his executors to sing Placebo, Dirige, &c. In the correspondence of Thomas, Lord Cromwell, one in 1536 is mentioned at which a hundred priests took part in the mass. Commemorative sermons were usually preached, the earliest printed example being one delivered by John Fisher, bishop of Rochester, on Margaret, countess of Richmond and Derby, in 1509.*

Source of Above: "Month's Mind." 1911 *Encyclopædia Britannica.* WikiSource. Accessed 20 June 2022.

https://en.wikisource.org/wiki/1911_Encyclopædia_Britannica/
Month%27s_Mind

197

KEEP

How are they set?

NEEDLE

At the board's end My Lady — 25

KEEP

And my young mistress by her?

NEEDLE

Yes. The parson
On the right hand (as he'll not lose his place
For thrusting) and 'gainst him Mistress Polish.
Next, Sir Diaphanous against Sir Moth:
Knights, one again another. Then the soldier, 30
The man of war, and man of peace, the lawyer;
Then the pert doctor and the politic Bias,
And Master Compass circumscribeth all.

(3.1.25-33)

Source of Above:

The Cambridge Edition of the Works of Ben Jonson. Volume 2. P. 470.

For Your Information:

I've chosen to draw on Fabritio Caroso's "Nobilita di Dame" (1600) in his Dialog Between a Disciple and His Master, on the Conduct Required of Gentlemen and Ladies at a Ball and Elsewhere for some pointers on how to behave in court.

[...]

Guests were led into the dining chamber in order of precedence. In a great hall, seats were usually laid out in a U-shape, with the lord at the base of the U. The most honored position was to the right of the lord, and the lowest at the bottom of the tables to the left of the lord.

It was important to wash hands before a meal. This might be done on the way into the hall, at a ewery board. Servants might also bring a ewer and basin around to the guests to wash their hands. The servants themselves, particularly the carver and sewer, visibly washed their hands as well. The ritual hand-washing in the dining chamber was more symbolic than thorough, but guests were definitely expected to have washed well beforehand. Grace was then said before the meal was served.

Next, the dishes were brought in and laid in a very precise order on the table, presentation being very important. Dishes were brought first to the high table, and then to the rest of the diners. Dishes requiring carving might be carried to a sideboard for carving. There were typically vast numbers of different dishes, but unlike modern feasts where everyone is expected to get a serving of every dish in a meal, not every dish would be within reach of every diner. Diners were expect[ed] to pick the things they liked best from the "messe" that was within reach of them. A messe is a set of dishes usually shared between 2-4 people.

Source of Above: "Elizabethan Manners." La tour du Lac, v2. Accessed 21 June 2022.

http://www.latourdulac.com/manners/Elizabethan.html

From the Bibliography:

Fabritio Caroso, *Courtly Dance of the Renaissance, a New Translation and Edition of the Nobilta di Dame (1600),* trans. Julia Sutton, Dover Publications, NY.

— 3.5 —

COMPASS

[To Practice] Yes, he has read the town. Towntop's his author!

(3.5.113)

Source of Above:

The Cambridge Edition of the Works of Ben Jonson. Volume 2. P. 487.

For Your Information:

The last top whipping master

"Whipping top" is a traditional game dating from ancient times that still enjoys great popularity in southern China. The residents in Daxi, Taiwan used to play whipping tops as kids, and the town itself is famous for producing king-sized versions of the toy. But these days, there's only one craftsman in town that can make them.

Source of Above: "The last top whipping master." CNTV. 11 April 2011
http://www.china.org.cn/video/2011-04/11/content_22333129.htm
Check out the photos on these pages:
http://www.china.org.cn/video/2011-04/11/content_22333129.htm
https://me.me/i/twelfth-night-act-1-scene-3-william-shakespeare-his-brains-turn-o-the-toe-like-a-lyrics-502bbe36073a4ee7aba67514ecf50b6f

— 3.5 —

DIAPHANOUS

Oh, you ha' read the play there, The New Inn
*Of Jonson's, that decries all other valour
But what is for the public.*
(3.5.92-94)
Source of Above:
The Cambridge Edition of the Works of Ben Jonson. Volume 2. P. 487.
LOVEL
*So help me Love, and my good sword at need!
It is the greatest virtue, and the safety
Of all mankind; the object of it is danger.
A certain mean 'twixt fear and confidence:
No inconsiderate rashness, or vain appetite
Of false encount'ring formidable things;
But a true science of distinguishing
What's good or evil. It springs out of reason,
And tends to perfect honesty; the scope
Is always honour and the public good:
It is no valour for a private cause.*
(*The New Inn* 4.4)
Source of Above:
The Cambridge Edition of the Works of Ben Jonson. Volume 6. P. 279.

— 3.5 —

COMPASS

This is a valour 145
I should desire much to see encouraged,
As being a special entertainment
For our rogue people, and make oft good sport
Unto 'em from the gallows to the ground.
(3.5.145-149)
Source of Above:
The Cambridge Edition of the Works of Ben Jonson. Volume 2. P. 489.
For Your Information:

Here's the actual text of the English law (on the books until 1870) outlining the death sentence for anyone convicted of high treason:

That you be drawn on a hurdle to the place of execution where you shall be hanged by the neck and being alive cut down, your privy members shall be cut off and your bowels taken out and burned before you, your head severed from your body and your body divided into four quarters to be disposed of at the King's pleasure.

Source of Above: Dave Roos, "The 'Hanged, Drawn and Quartered' Execution Was Even Worse than You Think." HowStuff Works. 29 June 2021

https://history.howstuffworks.com/history-vs-myth/hanging-drawing-and-quartering.htm

Note by David Bruce: Given the word order of "hung, drawn, and quartered," it seems plausible that "drawn" refers to the intestines being drawn out of the body.

— **4.7** —

We shall mar all if once we ope the mysteries
  O'the tiring house and tell what's done within:
  No theatres are more cheated with appearances,
  Or these shop-lights, than th'age's, and folk in them, 45
  That seem most curious.
(4.7.42-46)
Source of Above:
The Cambridge Edition of the Works of Ben Jonson. Volume 2. P. 509.

Ruth St. Denis was accustomed to improvise on stage, and frequently did not memorize the steps of her dances. During her duet with husband Ted Shawn in Josephine and Hippolyte, they smiled at each other and talked together throughout the dance. The audience thought they were making love talk at each other; instead, she was saying things such as "Teddy, what do I do next?" Mr. Shawn was saying things such as, "Ruthie, take six steps stage right, turn, look, hold out your arm and I'll come back to tell you what's after that."

Above Retold from this Source: Walter Terry, *Ted Shawn: Father of American Dance*, pp. 115-116.

<h1 style="text-align:center">— 4.8 —</h1>

COMPASS

As true it is, lady, lady, i'th'song.

(4.8.72)

Source of Above:

The Cambridge Edition of the Works of Ben Jonson. Volume 2. P. 513.

For Your Information: Here is a discussion of the lyrics:

https://mudcat.org/thread.cfm?threadid=79610

Here is the Book of Susanna, Chapter 1:

https://www.kingjamesbibleonline.org/Susanna-Chapter-1/

— 5.7 —

When he hath uttered all that you would know of him,
   I'll cleanse him with a pill as small as a pease
   And stop his mouth, for there his issue lies
   Between the muscles o'the tongue.
(5.7.57-60)
Source of Above:
The Cambridge Edition of the Works of Ben Jonson. Volume 2. P. 528.
Here is some information about the muscles of the tongue:

The tongue is all muscle, but not just one muscle — it's made up of 8 different muscles that intertwine with each other creating a flexible matrix, much like an elephant's trunk. It's called a muscular hydrostat, and the tongue muscles are the only muscles in the human body that work independently of the skeleton. Your tongue muscles do have amazing stamina and are used constantly for eating, talking, and swallowing. The tongue just never seems to get tired!

Source of Above: "10 Fun Facts About Your Tongue and Taste Buds." Reviewed By: Charles Patrick Davis, MD, PhD. Reviewed on 5/14/2021. MedicineNet.

https://www.medicinenet.com/fun_facts_about_tongue_and_taste_buds_slideshow/article.htm

Doctor, proceed with your cure. I'll make thee famous, 65
   Famous among the sons of the physicians,
   Machaon, Podalirius, Aesculapius.
   Thou shalt have a golden beard as well as he had,
   And thy Tim Item here have one of silver,
   A livery beard.
(5.7.65-70)
Source of Above:
The Cambridge Edition of the Works of Ben Jonson. Volume 2. P. 528-529.
Here is some information about Aesculapius' golden beard:

> *Dionysius, the tyrant of Syracuse, thought fit to accompany his thefts from temples with witty remarks. ... When he ordered the golden beard to be detached from the statue of Asclepius at Epidaurus, he declared that it was not appropriate for Asclepius to have a beard, given that his father, Apollo, was beardless (Valerius Maximus, Memorable Deeds and Sayings 1.1 ext. 3).*

Source of Above: "Asclepius and Healing Sanctuaries." The Hippocrates Code[1]: Unraveling the Ancient Mysteries of Modern Medical Terminology. Accessed 29 June 2022.
http://hippocratescode.com/asclepius-healing-sanctuaries/
Here is another translation:

> *But why should manners be judged by nationality? Masinissa, brought up in the midst of a barbarians, undid another man's sacrilege; but Dionysius, born at Syracuse, used to make jests of his sacrileges, of which he committed more than we have now room to recount: for having plundered the temple of Proserpina at Locri, and sailing upon the sea with a prosperous gale, laughing to his friends, he said, "What a pleasant voyage have the gods granted to us sacrilegious robbers!" Having taken also a golden cloak of great weight from Olympian*

---

1.   http://hippocratescode.com/

Jupiter, which Hieron the tyrant had dedicated to him out of the spoils of the Carthaginians; and throwing over the statue a woollen mantle, told his companions that a cloak of gold was too heavy in the summer, too cold in the winter; but a woollen cloak would serve for both seasons. The same person commanded the golden beard of Aesculapius to be taken from his statue in his temple at Epidaurus, saying that it was not appropriate for Apollo the father to be without a beard, and the son to have so large a one. He also took away the silver and golden tables [tablets] out of other temples, where finding certain inscriptions, after the manner of Greece, that they belonged to the good gods, then said he, "Through their goodness we will make use of them." He also took away the little statues of Victory, cups and crowns which they held in their hands being all of gold, saying that he did but borrow them, not take them quite away, saying that was an idle thing, when we pray to the gods for good things, not to accept them when they hold them forth to us. Who in his own person though he was not punished according to his deserts, yet in the infamy of his son, he suffered after death what in his life-time he had escaped. For divine anger proceeds at a slow pace to avenge itself, and compensates for the slowness with the gravity of the punishment.

Source of Above:

Valerius Maximus, *Factorum ac dictorum memorabilium libri IX* ("Nine books of memorable deeds and sayings"). Book 1: Of Religion. Adapted from the translation by S. Speed (1678). Accessed 29 June 2022.

http://www.attalus.org/translate/valerius1a.html

The same anecdote is told by Cicero:

He also gave orders for the removal of the golden beard of Aesculapius at Epidaurus, saying it was not fitting for the son to wear a beard when his father appeared in all his temples beardless.

Source: Cicero, *De Natura Deorum*, Book 3.83. Loeb Classical Library. 1933. In the Public Domain. Accessed 29 June 2022.

https://penelope.uchicago.edu/Thayer/E/Roman/Texts/Cicero/
de_Natura_Deorum/3B*.html#83

APPENDIX A: FAIR USE

This communication uses information that I have downloaded and adapted from the WWW. I will not make a dime from it. The use of this information is consistent with fair use:

§ 107. Limitations on exclusive rights: Fair use

Release date: 2004-04-30

Notwithstanding the provisions of sections 106 and 106A, the fair use of a copyrighted work, including such use by reproduction in copies or phonorecords or by any other means specified by that section, for purposes such as criticism, comment, news reporting, teaching (including multiple copies for classroom use), scholarship, or research, is not an infringement of copyright. In determining whether the use made of a work in any particular case is a fair use the factors to be considered shall include —

(1) the purpose and character of the use, including whether such use is of a commercial nature or is for nonprofit educational purposes;

(2) the nature of the copyrighted work;

(3) the amount and substantiality of the portion used in relation to the copyrighted work as a whole; and

(4) the effect of the use upon the potential market for or value of the copyrighted work.

The fact that a work is unpublished shall not itself bar a finding of fair use if such finding is made upon consideration of all the above factors.

Source of Fair Use information:

<http://www.law.cornell.edu/uscode/17/107.html>

I assume these things:

Everyone wants Good Samaritans to get credit for their good deeds, and this book about Good Samaritans is a good way to do that.

People who post on Imgur and Reddit or write letters to the editors want to share their information with the world.

Credit must be given where credit is due. I definitely try to do this.

I must not make money from this book.

APPENDIX B: ABOUT THE AUTHOR

It was a dark and stormy night. Suddenly a cry rang out, and on a hot summer night in 1954, Josephine, wife of Carl Bruce, gave birth to a boy — me. Unfortunately, this young married couple allowed Reuben Saturday, Josephine's brother, to name their first-born. Reuben, aka "The Joker," decided that Bruce was a nice name, so he decided to name me Bruce Bruce. I have gone by my middle name — David — ever since.

Being named Bruce David Bruce hasn't been all bad. Bank tellers remember me very quickly, so I don't often have to show an ID. It can be fun in charades, also. When I was a counselor as a teenager at Camp Echoing Hills in Warsaw, Ohio, a fellow counselor gave the signs for "sounds like" and "two words," then she pointed to a bruise on her leg twice. Bruise Bruise? Oh yeah, Bruce Bruce is the answer!

Uncle Reuben, by the way, gave me a haircut when I was in kindergarten. He cut my hair short and shaved a small bald spot on the back of my head. My mother wouldn't let me go to school until the bald spot grew out again.

Of all my brothers and sisters (six in all), I am the only transplant to Athens, Ohio. I was born in Newark, Ohio, and have lived all around Southeastern Ohio. However, I moved to Athens to go to Ohio University and have never left.

At Ohio U, I never could make up my mind whether to major in English or Philosophy, so I got a bachelor's degree with a double major in both areas, then I added a Master of Arts degree in English and a Master of Arts degree in Philosophy. Yes, I have my MAMA degree.

Currently, and for a long time to come (I eat fruits and veggies), I am spending my retirement writing books such as *Nadia Comaneci: Perfect 10*, *The Funniest People in Comedy*, *Homer's* Iliad: *A Retelling in Prose*, and *William Shakespeare's* Hamlet: *A Retelling in Prose*.

By the way, my sister Brenda Kennedy writes romances such as *A New Beginning* and *Shattered Dreams*.

APPENDIX C: SOME BOOKS BY DAVID BRUCE

Retellings of a Classic Work of Literature

Arden of Faversham: *A Retelling*

Ben Jonson's The Alchemist: *A Retelling*

Ben Jonson's The Arraignment, or Poetaster: *A Retelling*

Ben Jonson's Bartholomew Fair: *A Retelling*

Ben Jonson's The Case is Altered: *A Retelling*

Ben Jonson's Catiline's Conspiracy: *A Retelling*

Ben Jonson's The Devil is an Ass: *A Retelling*

Ben Jonson's Epicene: *A Retelling*

Ben Jonson's Every Man in His Humor: *A Retelling*

Ben Jonson's Every Man Out of His Humor: *A Retelling*

Ben Jonson's The Fountain of Self-Love, or Cynthia's Revels: *A Retelling*

Ben Jonson's The Magnetic Lady, or Humors Reconciled: *A Retelling*

Ben Jonson's The New Inn, or The Light Heart: *A Retelling*

Ben Jonson's Sejanus' Fall: *A Retelling*

Ben Jonson's The Staple of News: *A Retelling*

Ben Jonson's A Tale of a Tub: *A Retelling*

Ben Jonson's Volpone, or the Fox: *A Retelling*

Christopher Marlowe's Complete Plays: Retellings

Christopher Marlowe's Dido, Queen of Carthage: *A Retelling*

Christopher Marlowe's Doctor Faustus: *Retellings of the 1604 A-Text and of the 1616 B-Text*

Christopher Marlowe's Edward II: *A Retelling*

Christopher Marlowe's The Massacre at Paris: *A Retelling*

Christopher Marlowe's The Rich Jew of Malta: *A Retelling*

Christopher Marlowe's Tamburlaine, Parts 1 and 2: *Retellings*

Dante's Divine Comedy: *A Retelling in Prose*

Dante's Inferno: *A Retelling in Prose*

Dante's Purgatory: *A Retelling in Prose*

Dante's Paradise: *A Retelling in Prose*

The Famous Victories of Henry V: *A Retelling*

From the Iliad *to the* Odyssey: *A Retelling in Prose of Quintus of Smyrna's* Posthomerica

George Chapman, Ben Jonson, and John Marston's Eastward Ho! *A Retelling*

George Peele's The Arraignment of Paris: *A Retelling*

George Peele's The Battle of Alcazar: *A Retelling*

George Peele's David and Bathsheba, and the Tragedy of Absalom: *A Retelling*

George Peele's Edward I: *A Retelling*

George Peele's The Old Wives' Tale: *A Retelling*

George-a-Greene: *A Retelling*

The History of King Leir: *A Retelling*

Homer's Iliad: *A Retelling in Prose*

Homer's Odyssey: *A Retelling in Prose*

J.W. Gent.'s The Valiant Scot: *A Retelling*

Jason and the Argonauts: A Retelling in Prose of Apollonius of Rhodes' Argonautica

John Ford: Eight Plays Translated into Modern English

John Ford's The Broken Heart: *A Retelling*

John Ford's The Fancies, Chaste and Noble: *A Retelling*

John Ford's The Lady's Trial: *A Retelling*

John Ford's The Lover's Melancholy: *A Retelling*

John Ford's Love's Sacrifice: *A Retelling*

John Ford's Perkin Warbeck: *A Retelling*

John Ford's The Queen: *A Retelling*

John Ford's 'Tis Pity She's a Whore: *A Retelling*

John Lyly's Campaspe: *A Retelling*

John Lyly's Endymion, The Man in the Moon: *A Retelling*

John Lyly's Galatea: *A Retelling*

John Lyly's Love's Metamorphosis: *A Retelling*

John Lyly's Midas: *A Retelling*

John Lyly's Mother Bombie: *A Retelling*

John Lyly's Sappho and Phao: *A Retelling*

John Lyly's The Woman in the Moon: *A Retelling*

John Webster's The White Devil: *A Retelling*

King Edward III: *A Retelling*

Mankind: *A Medieval Morality Play* (A Retelling)

Margaret Cavendish's The Unnatural Tragedy: *A Retelling*

The Merry Devil of Edmonton: *A Retelling*

The Summoning of Everyman: *A Medieval Morality Play* (A Retelling)

Robert Greene's Friar Bacon and Friar Bungay: *A Retelling*

The Taming of a Shrew: *A Retelling*

Tarlton's Jests: A Retelling

Thomas Middleton's A Chaste Maid in Cheapside: *A Retelling*

Thomas Middleton's Women Beware Women: *A Retelling*

Thomas Middleton and Thomas Dekker's The Roaring Girl: *A Retelling*

Thomas Middleton and William Rowley's The Changeling: *A Retelling*

The Trojan War and Its Aftermath: Four Ancient Epic Poems

Virgil's Aeneid: *A Retelling in Prose*

William Shakespeare's 5 Late Romances: Retellings in Prose

William Shakespeare's 10 Histories: Retellings in Prose

William Shakespeare's 11 Tragedies: Retellings in Prose

William Shakespeare's 12 Comedies: Retellings in Prose

William Shakespeare's 38 Plays: Retellings in Prose
William Shakespeare's 1 Henry IV, aka Henry IV, Part 1: *A Retelling in Prose*
William Shakespeare's 2 Henry IV, aka Henry IV, Part 2: *A Retelling in Prose*
William Shakespeare's 1 Henry VI, aka Henry VI, Part 1: *A Retelling in Prose*
William Shakespeare's 2 Henry VI, aka Henry VI, Part 2: *A Retelling in Prose*
William Shakespeare's 3 Henry VI, aka Henry VI, Part 3: *A Retelling in Prose*
William Shakespeare's All's Well that Ends Well: *A Retelling in Prose*
William Shakespeare's Antony and Cleopatra: *A Retelling in Prose*
William Shakespeare's As You Like It: *A Retelling in Prose*
William Shakespeare's The Comedy of Errors: *A Retelling in Prose*
William Shakespeare's Coriolanus: *A Retelling in Prose*
William Shakespeare's Cymbeline: *A Retelling in Prose*
William Shakespeare's Hamlet: *A Retelling in Prose*
William Shakespeare's Henry V: *A Retelling in Prose*
William Shakespeare's Henry VIII: *A Retelling in Prose*
William Shakespeare's Julius Caesar: *A Retelling in Prose*
William Shakespeare's King John: *A Retelling in Prose*
William Shakespeare's King Lear: *A Retelling in Prose*
William Shakespeare's Love's Labor's Lost: *A Retelling in Prose*
William Shakespeare's Macbeth: *A Retelling in Prose*
William Shakespeare's Measure for Measure: *A Retelling in Prose*
William Shakespeare's The Merchant of Venice: *A Retelling in Prose*
William Shakespeare's The Merry Wives of Windsor: *A Retelling in Prose*
William Shakespeare's A Midsummer Night's Dream: *A Retelling in Prose*
William Shakespeare's Much Ado About Nothing: *A Retelling in Prose*
William Shakespeare's Othello: *A Retelling in Prose*
William Shakespeare's Pericles, Prince of Tyre: *A Retelling in Prose*
William Shakespeare's Richard II: *A Retelling in Prose*
William Shakespeare's Richard III: *A Retelling in Prose*
William Shakespeare's Romeo and Juliet: *A Retelling in Prose*
William Shakespeare's The Taming of the Shrew: *A Retelling in Prose*
William Shakespeare's The Tempest: *A Retelling in Prose*
William Shakespeare's Timon of Athens: *A Retelling in Prose*
William Shakespeare's Titus Andronicus: *A Retelling in Prose*
William Shakespeare's Troilus and Cressida: *A Retelling in Prose*
William Shakespeare's Twelfth Night: *A Retelling in Prose*
William Shakespeare's The Two Gentlemen of Verona: *A Retelling in Prose*
William Shakespeare's The Two Noble Kinsmen: *A Retelling in Prose*
William Shakespeare's The Winter's Tale: *A Retelling in Prose*